THERE WAS NO TIME LEFT!

John Rourke turned his back to the mountain, his gloved hand finding the butt of the Detonics mini gun under his armpit, ripping it free from the Alessi leather, his thumb jacking back the hammer.

A hail of assault rifle fire from the two climbers below tore into the rock face around him. Rourke stabbed the Detonics .45 toward the crampons from which the rope of the climbers was suspended — the rope vibrating under the weight of the climbers who clung to it. His finger twitched against the trigger, the little stainless steel pistol recoiled, the crampons suddenly rocketing away from the mountainside, the rope snaking outward, a scream from below as the two men fell away into the dark abyss.

John Rourke could only close his eyes, his head sagging against the cold rock face.

#16 THE ARSENAL

JERRY AHERN

ZEBRA BOOKS
KENSINGTON PUBLISHING CORP.

ZEBRA BOOKS

are published by

Kensington Publishing Corp.
475 Park Avenue South
New York, NY 10016

First printing: May, 1988

Printed in the United States of America

For our old pal Neal James — best wishes for everything. . .

CHAPTER ONE

John Rourke opened his eyes but remained perfectly still. The sound he had heard — a footfall in the sitting room outside their bedroom? But more than that. As if something had bumped against a wall or piece of furniture. Instantly, but so slowly that if he were being watched it would be virtually imperceptible, his right hand started to drift from over his abdomen where it had lain as he awakened. A smile crossed his lips — "things that go bump in the night." Sometimes pleasant, sometimes deadly.

His relationship with Sarah had sometimes been very pleasant and was so again. In the days before their marriage had started having the problems that had almost but not quite split them apart forever, Sarah had joked with him often about how waking him up in the morning could be so difficult; yet, if there were the slightest out-of-the-ordinary night sound, he would come instantly awake, instantly alert.

John Rourke told his wife that he didn't know why his mind and body worked that way, but was glad that they did; that perhaps it was some primordial response in the human subconscious that was only triggered by potential danger. Predatory animals had it and man was a predator. Like the big cats that had once prowled the earth, man found himself a lair, a secure place to sleep, to nurture his young, to dial down but never turn off those instincts which kept him alive in the world outside.

Sarah slept beside him now, on her back, her head turned to the side, facing toward him, her eyelids moving once as he looked at her out of the far left edge of his peripheral vision. The light sheet which covered their bodies outlined the still comparatively slight engorgement of her breasts, the more noticeable enlargement of her abdomen. She was nearly through the first trimester of her pregnancy.

He had never slept with a gun under his pillow with any degree of regularity for the simple fact that guns, no matter how small or how flat, were hard and contributed to a restless sleep. But he had developed the habit years ago of sleeping with a gun in instant reach of his hand, whether on a nightstand beside his bed, inside his sleeping bag or tucked into a shoe or boot beside him. His hand was still drifting. Slowly now, John Rourke moved his right hand and arm over the edge of the bed toward the leather sandals he had worn earlier in the evening after removing his combat boots. One of the twin stainless Detonics .45s was resting just inside the right one and the distended fingers of his right hand touched at the worn surface of the black checkered rubber Pachmayr grips.

Even though the Chinese were exceedingly friendly, were in fact allies against the Soviet forces, this suite of rooms in the Chairman's formal residence was not The Retreat and so he had kept the little Detonics Combat Master chamber loaded as was its twin on the seat of the high fan-backed "Sidney Greenstreet" chair a few paces across the room. His right fist closed over the pistol and he kept his arm motionless for an instant longer.

Another sound—this a footfall certainly.

His right arm flexed and he drew the pistol up beside him, his right thumb over the short spur of the hammer, his fist closed tight around the butt. He coughed and rolled over slightly, manufacturing sound to mask the telltale clicking as he drew the little .45's hammer from rest to full cock. He moved his legs quickly now—out of the bed, onto his bare feet, the pistol in his right fist shifting into his left so he could keep the muzzle toward the open doorway connecting the bedroom to the sitting room just beyond.

In two strides he was to the chair, his right fist closing over the butt of the second Detonics, his thumb drawing the hammer to full stand as he brought the muzzle up. He glanced at Sarah on the bed. If he awakened her, she might be in greater danger. And if his ears were playing tricks on his survival instincts, all the better reason not to arouse her—yet.

He moved toward the door, naked still, no time to skin into his pants.

Logic in such a situation as this dictated letting the intruder come to you. But if there were indeed an intruder or intruders, he could not let them come so close that Sarah and the baby in her womb would be in jeopardy.

John Rourke stood at the doorway. He held his breath. He listened.

He heard nothing. But he felt something without physically feeling it, the sixth sense so often spoken of almost fearfully, as if it were a touch of the unknown.

He backed toward the bed in long, quick strides, realizing he must make logic fit the situation. Cocked and locked, he set the Detonics from his right fist beside his right knee as he slipped onto the bed, his right hand closing over Sarah's mouth, her eyes opening instantly as she inhaled. He touched the trigger finger of his left hand to his lips and she blinked her eyes wide to indicate that she understood. Slowly, he moved his hand away from her mouth. She started to sit up, looking at him quizzically in the semi-darkness. He nodded and leaned back, both pistols in his fists again as Sarah rose slowly and eased out from beneath the sheet. She moved normally, not yet restricted by the baby. Her right hand moved to the bedside table and he could make out the Detonics-like shape of her Trapper Scorpion .45.

Rourke eyed the doorway, then gestured toward the bathroom. His wife shook her head vigorously. He gestured toward the bathroom again and after an instant's hesitation, she nodded and, barefoot, her ankle-length nightgown gathered up in her left hand, her pistol in her right, started for the bathroom.

John Rourke moved across the bedroom toward the chest of drawers. It was made of a type of metal that seemed reasonably heavy and cosmetically resembled wood. He crouched behind it, waiting. Before The Night of The War, when he had traveled considerably teaching survivalism and weapons training, he had spent many nights in hotel rooms across the world and continued the practice he had begun when he had gone on his first overseas assignment as what was euphemistically called a "case officer" for the United States Central Intelligence Agency. Immediately upon entering a room, if for some reason he was forced to travel unarmed, find suitable objects within the room that could be utilized as impromptu weapons — a lamp cord garrote, a complimentary magazine or newspaper that could be rolled tightly and used as a thrusting implement, an easily removed flushtank lid that could be used as an effective bludgeon, however unwieldy. It would only need to be used once. But when he was armed, which had been most of the time, the first order of business, after the usual thing of checking locks, fire and emergency escape routes and the like, was to select the best defensive position the room afforded. And it would usually devolve to a dresser or chest of drawers. Hotel dressers were most often long and low, giving considerable material through which an enemy bullet would have to travel before reaching him, slowing it down or deflecting it or, in the older hotels with the more solidly built furniture, perhaps stopping it entirely; and low enough to shoot over in order to return fire. There had been no such dresser in this bedroom, but the chest of drawers had seemed at least marginally adequate.

His eyes were wide open in the gray light and he realized a possible tactical flaw, setting one of the pistols on the floor tiles beside him and reaching up slowly to the top of the dresser. He found his dark-lensed aviator style sunglasses and put them on, then took up the second pistol again.

The luminosity of his black-faced Rolex Submariner glowed dully green.

John Rourke waited.

There was a loud thudding sound and in the same instant three men burst through the open doorway and into the room, dark clad, each of them armed with what looked like submachineguns or bullpup assault rifles, spotlights locked beneath them, flicking on, bathing the room in white light that would have momentarily blinded him if he hadn't thought of the sunglasses. They fired, the bullets from the automatic weapons in their hands ripping through the bed where only seconds before Sarah had lain. The furthest away of the three men in the room — John Rourke stabbed both twin Detonics pistols toward the man and fired, one round from each, slapping the man against the doorframe beside which he had been firing a split second earlier, his assault rifle still on full auto, spraying into the ceiling, the light secured beneath the gun dancing wildly. The second and third men started to turn toward Rourke now, but Rourke was already firing again, both pistols simultaneously, chunks of the ceiling raining down around them, the center man staggering back, the third man's body twisting right. Rourke had fired for the right side of the third

11

man's body so the impact of the 185-grain jacketed hollow point would push man and muzzle in the opposite direction from him. The light from the third man's weapon illuminated the first man's face for an instant. Rourke fired each pistol again as the first man slumped to the floor, his weapon silent, the other two men still firing. Rourke's shots impacted the second man in the upper portion of the chest or in the thorax. And the rolling beams from the flashes mounted beneath the weapons and the clouds of dust from the plaster-like substance which had made up the ceiling surface made visibility even worse, all movement as if in slow motion, jerky, like something out of an old silent film. Rourke's hit hammered the third man through the doorway and into the room beyond.

John Rourke was up, moving, three shots left in each pistol as he kicked the weapon away from the second man, sidestepped and impacted the heel of his left foot against the base of the man's nose. The fist man was clearly dead, eyes wide as Rourke caught a glimpse of the face in the light from the second rifle as it skidded across the floor.

Rourke stood beside the doorframe, listening. The third man had only one slug in him and might still be able to fire. Rourke thrust the pistol in his left fist through the doorway, not firing, but counting on attracting fire if the man were still capable of shooting.

There was no response.

Rourke dropped to his knees, a sticky wetness of blood against his bare skin. He caught up the man whose nose he had broken, then driven up into the brain, beneath the armpits, hauling him near, then pushing him erect along the doorframe as Rourke himself stood.

It was too dark to see faces clearly, even guess at the uniforms beyond the fact that they were dark-colored.

Maybe too dark to tell a naked man from one who was clothed. Rourke threw the body through the doorway and there was gunfire, Rourke throwing himself through the doorway after the already dead man, his eyes finding the muzzle flashes and as he came out of the roll, both pistols firing. There was a scream, a blast of automatic weapons fire into the floor and the sound of a body falling.

Two rounds remained in each of John Rourke's pistols.

He moved across the floor on knees and elbows, the tiles cold against his skin, his right elbow finding the wall beside the doorway.

Slowly, he raised to full height.

"John?" It was Sarah calling but he didn't answer her.

His right elbow flicked against the light switch and he threw himself toward where he remembered the couch to be, his left shoulder impacting it, his eyes tight shut for the instant the light came on, then opening as he rolled, squinted despite the dark lensed glasses.

There was no gunfire.

Both pistols preceded him from behind the couch.

The third man lay dead on the floor, the second man dead a few feet away. Rourke looked toward the doorway, seeing the booted foot of the first man.

It was a Russian boot, the kind issued to the KGB Elite Corps.

"John!"

"Stay where you are for a second—do it!" He walked toward the door between the suite and corridor, kicking away the third man's weapon. The door was partway open and he hit it with his right foot and it swung inward as he stepped back.

No enemy in the hallway.

A suicide assassination team. He could hear and as he removed his glasses now see Chinese guards running

13

from beyond the bend of the corridor toward the suite. Han, the Chinese Secret Service agent who had proven so valuable a man to his son and to himself, ran half-dressed at their lead. Rourke sagged back against the doorframe. The Russians had sent a suicide team into the First Chinese City—he and Sarah had been the targets.

"It's all right, Sarah!" Rourke shouted. But it wasn't all right at all.

And in the next instant she was beside him and taking his pistols from him so he could slip into a robe. Michael. Annie. Paul. Natalia. "Here—stay with Han," Rourke rasped, his left fist closing over Sarah's pistol, almost ripping it from her hand, the web of his own hand interposed between the hammer and the frame in case the trigger should trip.

His robe as yet untied, flying open, Rourke dodged into the corridor and sprinted down its length, Sarah screaming after him. "John!"

"Michael and Annie!" And as he glanced back, Rourke saw her, barefoot, her nightgown bunched up to her knees. Sarah was running after him. But in his mind he saw the surreal blueness of another woman's eyes . . .

The man was very tall and strongly built, the blond hair on his arms thick but little hair yet over his kidneys; but he was very young. Despite the fact of his youth, he might still prove an interesting match for the dogs.

The torches flickered. The Mongols fell silent. Mao's face was impassive but the bright blackness in his deep-set eyes betrayed the mixture of emotions which flowed surely through him now: pain and pleasure intermingled with pleasure from pain.

The man had been found wandering, wounded, and his wounds had been dressed and he had been given over

14

to Xaan-Chu. The man had revealed that he was a Russian ordinary soldier and that he had escaped following a terrible battle and wandered until the warriors had come upon him. The Russian had recounted his fright at the first sight of the martial Oriental visages and when Xaan-Chu had relayed that portion of the Russian soldier's account it had precipitated much laughter, however subdued. The mercenary class were indeed, at times, appalling in their appearance, ferocity of look and demeanor, something they cultivated as assiduously as the Maidens of The Sun cultivated quietness and civility and obedience; and, of course, their reflected radiance.

The man had recounted many strange tales, wondrous if they were to be believed and amusing at the least. And the motivation for his garrulousness seemed transparently obvious: he had deemed it impossible to resist the will of Xaan-Chu, perhaps too desiring to make himself important and therefore of sufficient value to ensure that his miserable life would be prolonged.

He could never have made himself that important.

Among the solider's stories had been one which had sounded most intriguing, however, and at once the least likely to contain even a grain of truth.

It was the tale of two men who had been enemies for five centuries. Their battle, of heroic proportions as the Russian soldier had told it, had begun in the short era which spanned the period between the Great War of Nuclear Annihilation and The Firestorm. The two men had both survived. One had been Russian and the other, also a mongrel, had been American. They had fought many battles, these two, and finally they fought their last battle.

That someone could have survived from the earlier period was hardly to be believed, but it made for a strange story. And the two characters in it — there were other characters to be sure woven into the soldier's tale, but of lesser importance — were interesting in the extreme. One had been named Vladmir Karamatsov and the Russian soldier had referred to him as "The Hero Marshal." The name of the other one, who survived the final battle between them, had been John Rourke, called "Doctor."

The self-proclaimed Russian soldier stood now beside the pit, his muscles rippling above and below the covering he had been given for his genitalia. Mao's eyes seemed unable to shift their gaze. The bandages were in place, still protecting the Russian's wounds. Yet, despite his imposing physique and the fact that he was a soldier and presumably had the benefit of some training in proper conduct in the face of death and, added to that, recent battle experience, when Xaan-Chu approached him and invited him to jump into the pit, he puddled the ground between his legs and attempted to cling to Xaan-Chu, crying like a woman.

But the Mongols moved forward at Xaan-Chu's subtle beckoning and with the butts of their rifles urged the Russian soldier to conduct himself in a more seemly fashion and hurtle his own body into the pit.

His initial fears apparently were swallowed within the universal instinct for survival and he fought well, using a tactic few would use although it was the best tactic to be sure. He took up an old human femur and utilized it as a weapon against the dogs. He injured one of the dogs and then the others brought him down; and, too quickly, it was over.

But such was increasingly often the case.

How would this Doctor, John Rourke, have fared? It would make interesting diversion for the bored or the idle to ponder . . .

John Rourke's right fist was balled tight on the butt of his wife's pistol as he slowed his headlong lunge, nearing the bend in the corridor on the opposite end of the Chairman's residence. The run had taken four minutes as he had judged it mentally, no time to look at his wristwatch, barely time to close the robe about his waist. The gunfire had aroused the various government functionaries who were occupying suites of offices throughout the building, the offices located at the massive building's center, the residential suites on its edges. And there had been more Chinese guards as well, recognizing him, following him to assist in whatever it was the nearly naked, pistol-wielding foreigner was busily hastening toward. Rourke smiled at the thought. He wondered if a man in a robe, carrying a pistol, running through the corridors of the pre-War White House would have been so trustingly received?

He glanced behind him, signalling the guards to cease their running as well, a dozen of them under the leadership of a slightly built young officer drawing up behind him. Rourke held a finger to his lips in the universal signal for silence, then advanced the few paces to the bend in the corridor, beyond which the apartments respectively shared by Annie and her husband Paul and Michael and his mistress Maria Leuden were located. And the suite in which Natalia slept alone. Like the corridor on the far opposite end of the building, its mouth was set with a circular couch covered in blue brocade, ornamental flowering shrubs arranged sparsely and tastefully in hand painted, tight waisted vases of black and blue and red lacquer, each gold rimmed and bearing the image of a single flower or only a barren branch. The corridor was wide and high ceilinged and softly lit. And John Rourke stepped into it now, his wife's pistol in his fist. There had been no sign of Sarah who had pursued him for the first minute or so

17

of his run, Han and his guards behind her. He imagined Sarah would be coming but there was no time to wait for her and if he found something very ugly it would be better if he found it first.

Revenge. It was the motive, of course. Natalia Tiemerovna had wielded the knife, but in the next instant he — Rourke — would have thrown both Vladmir Karamatsov and himself over the edge of the cliff to their deaths. To rid the world of Vladmir Karamatsov, John Rourke would have counted his own death a bargain. Karamatsov's forces there on the island had been killed or routed and his armies on the mainland had fled inland to regroup, perhaps under the leadership of one of his senior officers. And, though it would be likely that such an officer would welcome the ascent to power, such an officer would be bound by concerns for his image to attempt to avenge the Hero Marshal regardless of the cost in men or materiel. The Hero Marshal alive had been an unyielding enemy, a consummate evil. But dead, he was a holy martyr; and dead men were invincible.

The Chinese officer started to follow, with his lead element, into the corridor. John Rourke signaled the young man and his force back.

It was quiet. There was no sound. And it was possible that the sounds of gunfire had not pervaded here and that all was well. Possible. Unlikely. And Rolvaag and his dog, Hrothgar. The slightest sound which might not have stirred the Icelandic policeman would have stirred the animal who was always at Rolvaag's side.

John Rourke wiped his left palm against the side of his robe, along his thigh. He licked his lips. He started down the corridor, slowly, the Trapper Scorpion .45 cocked, safety downed, close at his right thigh.

Either everyone here was dead, or everyone here slept. Either there had been only one assassination squad, or there were two or more. And, if there were two or more and all here were not dead, then the additional team or teams had not yet struck, would be waiting, perhaps poised to kill at this very moment.

John Rourke stopped at the precise center of the corridor and stood, the gun still at his side. He raised his voice as loudly as he could and in Russian shouted, "John Rourke is alive. Your comrades in murder are dead. Which of you is hero enough to face me man against man? Or do you only lurk in cowardice to murder women in their beds? Three of your company fell to me. Because they were incompetent weaklings. Like you? Like the Hero Marshal who was so miserable a man that his own wife cut off his head? She should have cut off his testicles first, perhaps. Like yours are cut off." And then a man in black battle fatigues stepped from the doorway leading in to Natalia's rooms. He was tall, lean, in his left hand a submachinegun, his right hand sweeping the black BDU cap from his head, the hair blond beneath it but so close cut as to be hardly visible. He dropped the hat to the floor beside his feet, then bent his knees slightly and leaned the submachinegun against the door. The Russian commando's right hand moved slowly toward the pistol at his right hip.

Rourke shouted to the Chinese troops in what he realized was a poor rendition of their language but adequate to the task. "Do not interfere between this man and me!"

The Russian slowly moved the flap away from his holster, with his first finger — the trigger finger — and his thumb taking the weapon free of its confinement. He settled the pistol into a combat grip at his right thigh. He nodded curtly. John Rourke nodded back. The Russian's pistol was double action and the safety would be off. Cocked and locked, the Trapper gun Rourke held was more than an even match for the Russian's weapon.

19

Rourke spoke again in Russian. "The advantage is mine. So you go first. But one question. Are they still alive?"

"Yes. But when the first shot is fired, they die."

Rourke spoke so softly that his voice was almost a whisper. "You hold them prisoner?"

"A special gas was used. They are unconscious."

"Why was no gas used during the attack on my wife and myself?"

"It was the decision of the leader of the men who were to kill you. The Hero Marshal meant much to him. The wife of the Hero Marshal would never have betrayed the Hero Marshal had it not been for your seduction."

John Rourke felt the corners of his mouth downturning. Then he spoke again. "There is no need for your men to die. They can walk out of here alive and unmolested. That is my pledge if you order them to withdraw before they take the lives of my family. You can join them or stay and fight me. Whatever you wish."

"We all came, Doctor Rourke, knowing we would never leave."

John Rourke only nodded. When the first shot was fired, the executions of his daughter, his son, his best friend Paul, Natalia and Doctor Maria Leuden would begin.

"John! You can't—" It was Sarah, shrieking the words.

He kept his eyes on the Russian commando. In Chinese, he shouted, "Keep her back!" Then in Russian, he said, "Let us begin."

The bone leading across the back of the hand to the Russian's first knuckle—Rourke could see it vibrate slightly between the first and second dorsal interosseous as the trigger finger started to tense. John Rourke swept the Trapper Scorpion .45 up on a clean arc to just above waist level, his thumb wiping off the safety, his trigger finger flicking back once. Rourke was already racing toward the Russian commando as the Russian lurched backward along the corridor, his pistol discharging into the floor, his eyes wide open in death, blood gushing from his mouth.

Rourke shouted in Chinese, "Quickly! Into each room!" And subconsciously, he had already made his own choice. Michael was, after all, a man. And Natalia, the woman he loved like he had loved no other — but — He stepped into the open doorway of Annie and Paul's apartment, the residual smell of gas vaguely nauseating, seeing three men with submachineguns, seeing Annie and Paul still in their bed as though asleep, seeing all of it as though it were some tableau frozen in time, the submachineguns rising, one of the men turning toward the doorway into the corridor, another of the men turning away. The distance across the sitting room was fifteen feet. Rourke's right hand moved, the Trapper .45 bucking once in his fist as his right arm moved to maximum extension. He shot first at the man who was neither turning toward the doorway nor away, a chunk of flesh and bone beside the man's left ear bursting away from the head. Rourke's right arm arced right, toward the man turning away from the doorway. And Rourke fired, the bullet impacting the left eye. Rourke's right arm swung ninety degrees left and he fired again, the third man bringing his submachinegun on line toward Rourke. There was no time to dodge or duck or take cover. Rourke just fired, into the gaping open mouth of the third man, the head snapping back and the body going limp as the submachinegun opened up and cut a swatch across the far wall. Clinically, Rourke knew he had severed the third man's spinal column.

He dismissed the man mentally, the submachinegun still spraying into the wall as Rourke wheeled toward the doorway. The Scorpion had a six-round magazine and

Sarah loaded the chambered round off the top of the magazine just as he did with his Detonics pistols and that meant only two rounds were left.

He crossed the corridor, again choosing, he hoped, not for life or death. Michael and Maria Leuden — Natalia would have wanted him to do that.

The Chinese security people were nearly to the doorway of Michael's and Maria's apartment but Rourke was through the doorway first. Three men. Three submachineguns. All three pointed at the unconscious forms of Michael and Maria on the bed they shared. John Rourke stabbed the pistol toward the furthest of the three assassins and fired, the man's head snapping away and his body following it as the submachinegun sprayed across the wall and then into the headboard of Michael's and Maria's bed, the front of the assassin's face bloodied and deformed. Rourke moved the pistol left and fired at the second assassin, the right eye gone as the body slammed back against the wall and the submachinegun fell from his hands onto the bed. John Rourke was already running, hurtling himself toward the third man, the pistol, slide locked open, empty, turning in his right hand. As Rourke's body impacted the third man, Rourke's right hand hammered down, the butt of the handmade pistol smashing down along the crown of the skull and across the bridge of the submachinegunner's nose, Rourke's body slamming the man into the wall, the submachinegun between their bodies, discharging, Rourke's right knee slamming upward to find the groin, the thumb of his left hand puncturing the assassin's right eyeball, gouging and ripping, hooking, Rourke drawing the man's head toward him, then punching it into the wall, again and again and again, the submachinegun stilled, Rourke letting the body fall away, fluid from the eyeball mixed with blood, dripping from Rourke's left hand as he turned toward the bed. Michael and Maria

22

were unscathed.

Rourke heard submachinegunfire from the next suite of rooms — Natalia.

The nearest dead man's submachinegun. Rourke caught it up, jumping over the corpse as he ran toward the corridor, then toward the sound of the gunfire.

But it was already over.

Three black-clad Soviet commandos lay on the floor just beyond the bedroom doorway, clustered around Natalia. She lay on the bed. Rourke shoved his way past the Chinese guards, then sank to his knees beside her bed, his right hand abandoning the submachinegun, touching at her throat. There were no visible wounds. And his fingertips felt her pulse.

John Rourke closed his eyes for an instant, then ran from the room, into the corridor. Chinese guards milled about the entrance to the Bjorn Rolvaag's room. John Rourke shoved past them. Three of the black-clad commandos were dead on the floor. The huge dog, Hrothgar, lay at the foot of the bed; sprawled half out of the bed, a pool of blood around his face, was the Icelandic policeman. Rourke looked at the pistol in his hand. Its butt was matted with blood and hair. He set it down on the floor as he dropped to his bare knees beside the man.

The killing was done and it was time for other things.

CHAPTER TWO

He had seen too much of hospitals lately, John
Rourke thought. And he realized as he thought it that
such a thought was strange for a doctor. There had been
his own confinement and the virtually miraculous cura-
tive powers of the medical personnel at Mid-Wake.
There had been the time spent there while Michael and
Annie and Paul and Sarah and Natalia had all been
examined to see if, as it had been with him, the death of
radiation-linked cancer lurked within them as well. But
he had been the only one in whom it had been discovered and ever since it had been found and cured, he had
felt reborn. He had been near death when he had taken
a stomach full of assault rifle fire, lost great amounts of
blood, nearly expired from shock before anything else
could have claimed him. But as miraculously as the
medical personnel of Mid-Wake had saved him, he had
rapidly healed. Once it was safe to do so, he had begun a
regimen of physical exercise more strenuous than any he
had undertaken since the Awakening.

He had stayed at Mid-Wake for weeks afterward,
learning all he could of their advanced techniques, at his
side the German officer and physician, Doctor Munchen. Munchen had spoken of dire rumors heard of
Eden Base and the power struggle that was inexorably
leading to confrontation between Akiro Kurinami and
Commander Dodd.

What had struck John Rourke then and what he

pondered now as he waited in this Chinese hospital, his wife beside him, was that mankind had learned so little. The entire world had been nearly destroyed. Out of greed, envy and distrust. Greed, envy and distrust were growing again. And when they were again harvested, would the world this time survive?

He smoked one of the non-carcinogenic cigarettes the Germans made, the package taken from Natalia's suite. It was too confined here to smoke one of the thin, dark tobacco cigars that were his favorites.

The gas used to quell any possibility of resistance to the assassins was still being analyzed, both from blood samples taken from Annie, Paul, Michael, Maria and Natalia and from the unmarked cannisters found on the bodies of the dead Russians. The origin of both the gas and the men was frighteningly clear. Indeed, some one or more of Karamatsov's senior officers had taken charge of his armies and was leading them. Where? To what ends? It was vital that no link be allowed to form between the Soviet forces on land and those of the Soviet underwater complex which still battled the friendly forces of Mid-Wake in five centuries of unabated submarine warfare. Such a link would give the Soviets on land unlimited access to nuclear weapons. Already, Rourke suspected, the Germans would be working to produce nuclear weapons as a counter-measure to the missing elements of the Chinese nuclear arsenal should the land-based Soviet forces locate them.

History was repeating itself. Santayana had put it best: "Those who do not learn the lessons of history shall be forced to relive them." No one had learned the lessons as well as Sarah, Annie, Paul, Michael, Natalia and himself, the only six persons on earth who had lived through the era of the holocaust, discounting the few who had taken The Sleep with Karamatsov and who still served Karamatsov's memory. The Eden Project survivors had escaped earth the moment the thermonuclear nightmare had begun, returned to the ruins of earth only after its voracious appetite for death had been sated, its thirst for blood slaked. They had never known the death.

And this time, the earth's atmosphere was too delicate a fabric to withstand another assault. All life, all humankind, would perish.

"What are you thinking about? You should see your face. It looks like some sort of mask—rage, fury. What are you thinking, John?"

John Rourke looked at his wife. A voice was calling over the intercom in Chinese, summoning a doctor if his recently acquired yet still meager knowledge of Chinese served. Rourke said to her, "Some used to say that after a nuclear war, the living would envy the dead. Remember?"

"I remember."

Except for his wife and children and Natalia and himself, there was no one else who could have remembered.

The Chairman himself entered the waiting room, bowing deferentially to Rourke and his wife, then looking Rourke square in the eye as Rourke stood. The Chairman was an aesthetic looking man, tall and thin, immaculate, with penetrating eyes that showed neither hardness nor emotion. "I am pleased to report, Doctor Rourke, that our doctors indicate that the condition of your children, Mr. Rubenstein, Doctor Leuden and Major Tiemerovna improves by the minute. The effect of the gas, I am told, is merely temporary. Even now, your daughter is returning to consciousness. But I am also advised that it might be well to allow your daughter and the others to rest for some time lest they suffer from undue exertion. The Icelandic policeman, Rolvaag, is an exception. Although he was also gassed, apparently because of his great size, the gas took effect more slowly and he was subdued with a blow to the head. His condition is guarded. I took the liberty of anticipating that you might indeed have concern for the welfare of the dog which is his constant companion. The veterinary center relays the information that the animal is well."

Rourke was about to speak as the door into the waiting room opened again, the German Captain Otto Hammerschmidt entering, the shoulders of his uniform parka wet with melted snow, his blue eyes pinpoints of light as he doffed his cap and ran the fingers of his left hand back through his militarily short hair. "Herr Chairman. Herr Doctor Rourke. Frau Rourke. I have only just heard—"

The Chairman responded. "All are well, save for Mr. Rolvaag who has sustained head injuries and whose condition is guarded, Captain Hammerschmidt."

Before Hammerschmidt could speak, Rourke did. "What have your security people ascertained concerning the Russians who penetrated the First City, Mr. Chairman?"

"Several guards at the perimeter and at the tunnel were, unfortunately, liquidated barbarously. By this means, the interlopers were able to gain access to the Petals and to yours and your family's respective apartments. Steps have already been taken to increase the efficiency of the guard. But I fear this shall not be the last attempt on your persons."

"They've reorganized quickly," Hammerschmidt said under his breath, almost as though thinking aloud. "We ought to pay them back in kind, I think," Hammerschmidt added, raising his voice a little.

John Rourke looked at Hammerschmidt, saying nothing . . .

* * *

He had given Sarah a mild sedative that was safe for her to use even with her pregnancy, one of the drugs he had learned about at Mid-Wake. She had taken it under protest, but he had convinced her she needed the rest. Her pistol freshly loaded and left beside the bed, he left her, Chinese guards at the door of this new suite of rooms where she slept, their original apartment was a melange of the blood and gore and bullet holes, a memento of violence.

John Rourke sat in the small conference room, Otto Hammerschmidt opposite him across the black lacquer table. John Rourke lit the thin, dark tobacco cigar that he had kept clenched in his teeth since leaving Sarah asleep.

"I have the word that you sought from Colonel Mann, Herr Doctor."

"And?"

"Deiter Bern has authorized the production of nuclear weapons as a possible defensive measure against the armies of the Soviet."

"That's insanity."

Hammerschmidt's eyes flickered. "He has the welfare of all peoples at heart, Herr Doctor. I am also told that it is his full intention to share this technology with the personnel of Eden Base and with the Icelandics. It is only self-defense."

"And then with the Chinese eventually, I suppose?"

"I should assume so, Herr Doctor. Permit me." And he lit a cigarette, exhaling smoke in two thin streams from his nostrils. "If the Russians realize, Herr Doctor, that they cannot hope to win a full scale confrontation—"

"That philosophy didn't work five centuries ago. Although God knows rational men on both sides tried to make it work. This time there won't be any second chance."

"I was told, Herr Doctor, that Deiter Bern would most welcome personally discussing this with you at your convenience."

"That's very good of him, Hammerschmidt. Look— ahh—I know you and Michael are close friends. I didn't mean to put you in the middle of this. All of us consider you a friend. I had to know, though."

"It is for the good of all mankind, Herr Doctor. If whoever has taken over the leadership of Karamatsov's armies should find the remainder of the Chinese nuclear arsenal, or effect some sort of treaty with the Soviet forces based in the Pacific and thereby obtain nuclear weapons—it is unthinkable."

Rourke smiled at the word. "Unthinkable" had become reality five centuries before, which he supposed proved that just because something was unthinkable it wasn't undoable. "What if," Hammerschmidt continued, "this new Soviet force should decide to launch its missiles against us even as we speak?"

"The numbers of missile tubes aboard their submarines are optimistic at the moment. Only ten percent of those on the captured Island Class submarine were loaded with anything besides ballast." The captured submarine had been investigated from stem to stern, everything that could be disassembled, analyzed, reassembled, tested, stressed. As an ancillary benefit, since by coincidence it had been the same Island Class monster submarine by which he and Natalia had originally been taken against their will to the Soviet underwater complex, the Mid-Wake teams had also found his musette bag, his leather jacket, Natalia's holsters and the rest of their miscellaneous gear. "That's probably typical. And certainly that's a threat, and a serious one. And maybe that's the point. Just one or two nuclear explosions might do it this time. Burn the atmosphere

29

away so totally that the planet will die and no matter where you are or how well you've planned ahead, nothing will matter. There will never be a surface to return to. It almost happened before. This time it will happen. Your own scientists can tell you that."

"And what are we to do, Herr Doctor? Let the Soviets have all the thermonuclear missiles and then, when they make their demands, merely submit? We are free men now. You—better than anyone because you gave us our freedom—should appreciate that, Herr Doctor. What are we to do, then?"

John Rourke noticed that his cigar had gone out in his fingertips. He didn't answer Otto Hammerschmidt because there was no answer to give.

CHAPTER THREE

Natalia Anastasia Tiemerovna sat up in bed. She remembered it all in a rush and it sickened her. Or perhaps, she told herself, it was only the aftereffect of the gas.

There was a noise and she reached for the suppressor fitted Walther PPK/S beside her bed. The door into her bedroom opened as her hand closed over the black plastic grips. But already, gas was filtering across the room toward her, the cloud enveloping her as the men — how many had there been? she couldn't remember — had closed with her. She held her breath, but somehow — She remembered awakening here in the hospital and being told by someone that everyone was all right and she should rest. Without wanting to, she had closed her eyes. She closed them again as the tears came. Each day, they had come more and more . . .

John Rourke stood beside the Chinese doctor, a pretty woman dressed in nursing whites interpreting. "What is the nature of the injury to Mr. Rolvaag's head? May I see the X-rays?"

She spoke in rapid Chinese and the doctor nodded, took up a small gray paper envelope and withdrew a black plastic object about the size of a computer printer ribbon from the twentieth century, then walked toward the wall unit which looked like a flat, large screen video monitor. He inserted the black plastic object into a slot at the base of the screen and the screen came alive. First, there was a visual representation in the usual two dimensional X-ray format, unusual to a twentieth century trained doctor only in that the representation was in color. But he was used to that. Next, although he had seen it before, was something he doubted he would ever cease to marvel at. Like a computer diagram with the pixels being added in sequence to develop image, the cranial cavity of Bjorn Rolvaag began appearing as a rotating three dimensional laser hologram.

There was a hematoma visible near the inferior genu of the Fissure of Rolando. The nurse began translating again. "Doctor Su has preparations already begun for the lasering of this hematoma. It is a procedure similar to operations he has performed in the past and he anticipates good success and, barring complications, full recovery."

John Rourke looked away from the machine and at the red-haired giant unconscious on the bed. Rolvaag had saved his daughter's life. A silent man, close only to his dog, Rourke barely knew him. And if he were to die in this place so far from his native Lydveldid Island, it would be another in the mounting heap of random injustices since the Night of The War.

And that this bothered him, John Rourke realized, reaffirmed his own humanity.

Rourke walked to the bed, placed his hand on the Icelandic policeman's shoulder and whispered in the English which Rolvaag understood so little of, "It will be all right, Rolvaag. Your dog is well. All of us are well. You will be well, too. So rest for now."

Rourke stood beside the bed for a while, watching the man breathe.

CHAPTER FOUR

The shadows of the rotor blades, black against the alternating splotches of white and gray, became more pronounced, more solid, the machine subtly changing pitch to compensate for some errant crosswind (a regular condition here), then touching down with a barely noticeable sideways lurch. What little noise had been audible within the confines of the fuselage became for an instant totally imperceptible as the rotation rate radically dropped. But in the next second, the winding down whine could be heard as the fuselage door was slid open. And there was the sound of the wind which had assailed the machine. He unbuckled his harness and rose, then walked to midway along the helicopter's length, turned and stared out into the morning.

An Arctic Cat, a half-track truck, the tarp covering the bed turned back, a dozen men with assault rifles held at port—this was the reception honor guard. He smiled at the thought. His eyes drifted back to the truck bed. A heavy machinegun was implaced there surrounded by sandbags.

Trust was a wonderful thing, the total lack of trust self-evident here.

Colonel Nicolai Antonovitch, once Kremlin liaison officer for the KGB Elite Corps in the days prior to the Night of The War, before that subordinate to Natalia Anastasia Tiemerovna (faces passed fleetingly through his memory like phantoms since he had left China and begun the flight to the Urals, a flight at once into his past and his future), stepped down from the helicopter. He was now, in the absence of any challengers of sufficient influence, master of the armies once commanded by the Hero Marshal, Vladmir Karamatsov. Possessed of Karamatsov's armies, but by neither his jealousies nor his egotism.

It seemed there was always snow here, splotching the gravel and the shale which was like flaked gray skin from the mountain itself.

Antonovitch started walking, hunching his shoulders beneath the turned up collar of his dress uniform black greatcoat. When the wind gusted, it chilled him to the depths of his being. It had not been that long ago when the Hero Marshal, after four years of self-imposed exile, had returned here in triumph and anticipation. And in the whole scheme of things, precious little time for men born five centuries ago had passed between that day and Karamatsov's abortive bid for ultimate power over the Soviet people. There were, quite likely, wild creatures who would devour the womb which nurtured them.

So it had been with the Hero Marshal.

The wind shifted and Antonovitch's eyes involuntarily began to tear as he focused on the head of his welcoming committee. Yuri Vanyovitch waited a respectable distance beyond the outer redoubts of the Underground City. Much had changed with the defenses here, Antonovitch, drawing nearer, noticed with a militarily critical eye. Assistant to the party secretary, about Vanyovitch there was an air of importance — both genuine and assumed — well beyond his apparent youth.

"Assistant Secretary Vanyovitch. As always, Comrade, an honor," Antonovitch began, rendering a salute, not waiting for any return since Vanyovitch was a bureaucrat.

Vanyovitch smiled thinly. "Comrade Colonel Antonovitch. We were most startled at your communication."

No pleasantries, Antonovitch thought. He mentally shrugged. "You may be more startled by other news I have to tell." He gestured to the mountains beyond the level ground on which they stood. "And I imagine you know that German troops move about out there and monitor the Underground City."

"Did you come all this way to tell me that, Comrade Colonel?"

"Hardly. But I will tell my story to the First Secretary, Comrade. You may listen if it is his desire." Certain persons needed to be put in their place immediately. He had learned that — been put in his own place at times. Karamatsov had been his teacher. "Shall we?"

Vanyovitch said nothing, but turned and started to walk toward the Cat . . .

Michael Rourke waited at the monorail station, beside him only Maria Leuden, the monorail which had left a moment earlier carrying Annie and Paul to a different petal of the flower-shaped Chinese First City. "When I was a kid I rode a subway — at least once."

"A subway?"

"A train like this," he told her, "but it rode on two rails and if I remember correctly it received its electrical power from a third rail. I remember my father telling me that you never touch the third rail."

"Where was this?"

"Atlanta, I think. I couldn't have been more than a couple of years old. Five, maybe — tops."

"And Atlanta was the capitol of the province —"

"State. The state of Georgia. It was nuked, as they used to say, on the Night of The War. That was why we had to leave the farm. Even up there in northeast Georgia, we were uncomfortably close to Atlanta, the possibility of fallout, and the people who fled the city. All of that."

The train came — the monorail, he mentally corrected himself.

Her voice quiet, low-key as it usually was, Maria Leuden asked, "Do you think Natalia will be all right?"

"She'll be fine. Must have been a bad reaction to the gas, that's all. Artificially elevated her blood pressure. She'll be fine," and Michael Rourke stepped partially through the doorway to block it open for Maria as she passed through, then stepped after her and seated himself beside her, shifting his shoulders as if the double shoulder rig for the two Berettas were in place. But it wasn't. Being unarmed, even here, made him uncomfortable. Guns and knives had been an integral part of his daily existence since he was a little boy and the Night of The War came.

He looked at Maria's pretty green eyes and folded his arms around her shoulders. "Natalia'll be fine. Don't worry." Maria Leuden leaned her head against his left shoulder, but first touched her lips gently to his cheek.

Tension, his father had said. Tension was what was bothering Natalia Anastasia Tiemerovna . . .

Natalia looked up at him. She squatted cross-legged in the middle of the bed and the hint of circles under her eyes was dramatized by the contrast between the blueness of the eyes themselves and the whiteness of her skin.

"You need a rest," John Rourke told her.

"Maybe you can call a travel agent and arrange for me to have a few weeks in the Bahamas — or the Black Sea. Pretty much the same and the prices are cheaper at the Black Sea."

"I've been having some talks with the chief archivist here. Some of the clues to the whereabouts of the Third City that baffle present day Chinese seem to make sense to me with a Twentieth Century perspective. At least I think they do," Rourke smiled. "How about we take a few weeks and check it out."

"What about Sarah? The baby?"

"She'll be all right."

"You can't have one wife to make pregnant and one wife to go adventuring with, John." He didn't say anything. Natalia did again. "Did you tell Sarah I appear high strung? That a few weeks in the wild with me would get me calmed down and back to normal?"

"No."

"Did you tell her we'll wind up sleeping beside each other but never together?"

"No. I didn't tell her that."

"Vladmir's dead. These new Soviet commandos. Probably Antonovitch. He's the logical man. Served with Vladmir before the Night of The War, took the Sleep with him, served him faithfully afterward. He inherited by right."

"You told me he's rational."

"He's still KGB. He's not a sadist. He's not an egomaniac. At least he wasn't. But in his way, he's just as evil. But for practical ends. Not because it gets his rocks off. I'm tired," she concluded.

"I can come back."

"No. You don't have to go. I can't rest."

"What is it? Us?" Rourke asked her. Her hands shook as she tried lighting a cigarette and Rourke found the battered Zippo in the pocket of his Levis and rolled the striking wheel under his thumb, the blue-yellow flame flickering as Natalia drew it into the cigarette.

"There is no 'us', John. There can't be. There never could have been. Both of us have always known that. But

I'm Russian and Russians are so adept at tragedy. And I guess gods are too," and she looked him hard in the eyes.

"This is—"

"Self-defeating? If anyone recognizes what's self-defeating, it should be me. I mean, after all, I'm so experienced. Aren't I?" She didn't wait for an answer. "I used to think I'd be willing to die if once you made love to me. And do you—"

"Don't—"

"No—and the silly thing! I still feel that way. I'm crazy. That's what I am."

"You're not—this—"

"Crazy?"

Natalia had been (was she right?) this way since—and Rourke closed his eyes for an instant . . . Karamatsov crawled to his feet, staggered back, by the edge of the precipice over the sea.

Karamatsov's right hand shot forward and in his fist was the little snub-nosed Smith & Wesson revolver he had carried five centuries ago. "You are dead, John Rourke!"

John Rourke stood there, hands clutched to his abdomen, about to throw himself against Karamatsov and hurtle them both over the edge and into the sea on the rocks below.

And then he heard Natalia's voice. "No, Vladmir!" And she rose up beside Karamatsov and Karamatsov turned to look at her and in both her tiny fists she held the short-sword-sized Life Support System X and the steel moved in her hands over her head and around in an arc to her right and then—

The Crain knife stopped moving.

Karamatsov's body swayed.

The little revolver fell from his limp right hand.

His head separated from his neck and sailed outward into the void.

Blood sprayed geyser-like into the air around Karamatsov like a corona of light.

The headless torso of her husband rocked backward and was gone over the edge.

Natalia screamed . . . John Rourke opened his eyes. Natalia wasn't screaming at all, just staring at him. "The one thing I'm sure of and I wanted you to be sure of. I love you—and I know that's destroying you and if I could stop loving you and it would do any good, I would. Rest." John Rourke leaned over her, his hands holding her head gently, his lips touching her almost black hair. He could hear her starting to cry again . . .

The conference hall was the same as he remembered it. But that time, Vladmir Karamatsov had been seated at the head of the table. This time, he—Antonovitch—stood before it. Yuri Vanyovitch took the seat immediately on the left. To Antonovitch's right already sat Boris Korenikov, Principal Secretary.

Korenikov's voice might have made the uninitiated listener think Korenikov suffered from laryngitis.'But the voice was always that way, strained and tight and dry, as annoying to hear as the sound of fingernails drawn across a chalkboard. The corners of Korenikov's mouth downturned as he began to speak, slowly, laboriously, the mouth only serving to further draw out his already elongated face into an image reminiscent of a very sad, tired looking dog. "Comrade Colonel—or have you already taken to yourself the title 'Marshal'?"

An answer was called for, but he didn't know which answer to give.

There was silence punctuated only by one of the six ministers at the table clearing his throat. Antonovitch spoke. "If I viewed the world, Comrade First Secretary, as did the Hero Marshal, then I would be laying siege to the Underground City, not entering it to seek counsel and offer support."

"That is a very good answer, Colonel Antonovitch. How truthful—I have no wish to offend—we shall, however, see. And what counsel is it you seek?"

"Beneath the surface of the Pacific Ocean, there is a Soviet community of great strength and possessed of nuclear weapons. The Chinese are powerful and technologically sophisticated. There will soon be, if there is not already, an alliance formed between the existing alliance—the Germans, the Eden survivors, the Icelandics—and this new enemy, the Chinese. The Chinese may well have access to nuclear weapons beyond those which were lost to the Hero Marshal during a less than well-planned military adventure along the coast. The Germans have the ability to construct nuclear weapons—technologically. The Eden Project survivors may well have nuclear weapons stockpiled for their use which can be reactivated after five centuries and turned against us. The Soviet people here on the land have no nuclear weapons—yet. But they must be obtained or fabricated. The Soviet people have available to them the means to reactivate Particle Beam weaponry in a much shorter period of time than it would take for the Germans or the Chinese to develop such technology. The Soviet people, if our differences can be set aside, have available to them the largest and most fully equipped standing army on the face of the planet. I come to you seeking counsel concerning how our differences can be put aside for the good of the Soviet people whom we all serve."

There was silence, not even the clearing of a throat, then First Secretary Korenikov broke the silence. "Be seated, Comrade Marshal Antonovitch."

CHAPTER FIVE

The red light clicked off and Akiro Kurinami pressed his hands tightly over his eyes for a moment as defense against the brightness of the ordinary white light, then took his hands away. Outside, it was a starless night, the heavy overcast of snowladen clouds making the last stage of the trek up the mountainside like moving while hooded with black velvet. He felt like a sneak thief, but coming here was the only way to survive. And he knew John Rourke well enough that "the only way to survive" was, to John Rourke, a powerful argument, and if entering his sanctum unbidden would be viewed as a transgression at all, it would be forgiven.

Elaine Halversen squeezed his left hand and he looked down at her hand in his—the chocolate brown of her flesh. But he wondered why men of his race were called yellow, because despite his Japanese origins his hand looked white against hers. His eyes tracked upward from their hands to her eyes, as dark as his own, but somehow different, and very beautiful.

Together, they descended the three steps from the interior vault door into the great room of The Retreat.

Kurinami had half-hoped what Elaine's words echoed. "If he were only here!"

But The Retreat was empty, except for themselves, he realized, had realized from the moment they had opened the doors. He had once said to John Rourke, "Why haven't you shown Commander Dodd the location of The Retreat — it might prove important some day?"

And Rourke, taking the cigar from his mouth, the corners of his eyes — all that was visible with his eyes shielded by the dark lensed aviator-style sunglasses he habitually wore — wrinkling slightly as though he were smiling, said, "If someone knows a secret, then it's no longer a secret. Dodd could find The Retreat by working out the coordinates off the transmission logs of the Eden computer. But he'd have to blow the top of the mountain off to get inside unless he knew how. You and Elaine share a secret that no one outside my family knows. You're now just as responsible for the integrity of that secret as we are. I didn't intend to stick you with such a responsibility, but you were the first people we had seen. It just sort of happened."

Akiro Kurinami now thanked God that it had.

Exposure, lack of food, exhaustion and despair had nearly claimed them.

"If we're going to invade his home, we may as well invade his refrigerator," Elaine began, the cheerfulness of her tone sounding forced to him.

"Yes," he nodded, stripping away his arctic parka, dropping it on the floor of the great room. And he suddenly felt rude. He picked up the coat, holding it dumbly, looking for some place to hang it.

He had not eaten in two days, holding back the last of the emergency rations he had stolen — stolen? — for Elaine, giving them to her hours ago to keep her going.

After he had been kidnapped, tortured, nearly killed, escaping barely in time to save Elaine from that fate or worse, they had sought sanctuary among the Germans who helped to guard Eden Base, the Germans giving it gladly. But after an eternity of wrangling between Commander Dodd and German high command, it had appeared inevitable that he and Elaine would be surrendered. And so, stealing what he could for them, they fled.

He didn't blame the Germans. He and Elaine were victims of diplomacy and duplicity. The Germans had been faced with serious criminal charges, including various counts of murder, leveled against him by Commander Christopher Dodd, technically the leader of a foreign nation on whose soil the German base was located.

Elaine handed him a drink. It smelled like whiskey. It was whiskey as he tasted it.

He wondered if he had decided they should flee simply to obviate the necessity of the Germans doing what they at once thought was immoral but a moral imperative?

"Some of those irradiated steaks and frozen potatoes and vegetables that look like they were fresh—maybe ones Annie and Michael grew in the garden."

"You're too tired. You should rest. Just anything would—"

The whiskey warmed his stomach more than it had burnt his throat; so, admittedly never a connoisseur of spiritous liquor, he felt he had achieved a baseline for judgment that it was good.

She kissed him, hard on the mouth and he felt warmed more than the whiskey could have made him feel. "You either rest here or take a shower and warm up. Doctor's orders," she laughed.

She was a "doctor" but a PhD, not MD and it had become a running joke between them. "I declare martial law—so it's lieutenant's orders," he told her.

She kissed him again—this time on the cheek and moved off before his hands could react and he found himself laughing, something he had not done in the weeks since it had all started. He stood up, the whiskey hitting him now and making his balance a little uncer-

43

tain. Two days without food.

He left the rest of the whiskey and started up the three steps toward the bathroom, the door open.

The main computer aboard Eden One blanked out, robbing Eden survivors of the location of strategic stores.

Missing: twenty-four M-16 assault rifles, three thousand rounds of 5.56mm Ball, botanical samples, lighting, medical supplies, emergency rations.

The men and the electric shock torture so he would reveal the location of the backup files he had made for the main computers. These were still hidden.

Akiro Kurinami leaned over the wash basin and then looked up into the mirror.

Taped to the mirror was a computer printout, the letters daisy wheel quality rather than dot matrix.

"Akiro and Elaine:

It may strike you as odd that I have left this note for you, but you might well appreciate that only 'odd' circumstances would place you in a position to be reading it. My house, as they say, is your house. You know the location of weapons, food and medical supplies. If you have come here, circumstances are likely desperate. Remember that you are safe here if you kept the secret. Colonel Mann donated a wonderfully powerful radio transmitter which Michael and I have installed. I have no way of knowing what has prompted your visit. If you need help, you can trust Doctor Munchen. Contact him if you cannot contact me directly.

John Rourke

P.S. Don't attempt to ride the Harleys unless you are quite experienced with motorcycles. Forgive me that I neglected to ask."

Kurinami could see part of his own face in the mirror, beyond the edge of the letter. And his face seamed with a smile as he thought of John Rourke's often spoken motto, "It pays to plan ahead."

CHAPTER SIX

Han Lu Chen's eyes were intense bullets of blackness as the Chairman spoke, Rourke watching Han rather than the Chairman. "It has been suggested by the Germans, who even now seek to formalize an alliance between our peoples against the growing Soviet threat, that an embassy be sent to the Second City in the hopes of ending the centuries of philosophical differences which have divided us. Certainly, the possibility that the rulers of the Second City know the whereabouts of the remainder of the People's Republic's nuclear arsenal from before the Dragon Wind came and might make such weapons available to the Soviets, is a fact which cannot be ignored."

John Rourke shifted his eyes to Otto Hammerschmidt. Between the German commando captain and the Chinese intelligence agent Han sat his son, Michael. Michael caught his glance, raised his eyebrows in simulation of a shoulder shrug and looked away.

"Doctor Rourke," the Chairman began again, seating himself at last at the head of the long black lacquer table which was set like a piece of onyx in the immensity of the otherwise bare conference hall. "The people of Eden. What is their feeling?"

John Rourke studied the Chairman's face for a moment, then answered. "Sir; I cannot speak for the Eden Project, although I intend to return there soon. I would, however, be honored if you were to request that I carry

46

your good wishes and news of your interest in Eden leadership opinion. But, in candor, at the moment I have less in common with Eden leadership than I have had in the past. A valued friend, one Lieutenant Akiro Kurinami, has been charged with various heinous crimes and falsely so, I believe. Again, speaking frankly, I hold the current Eden leadership under Commander Dodd personally responsible. I've been exposed to his manipulation of justice before, and with nearly disastrous results." Natalia had almost been killed because of Dodd's ineptitude — or was it design? — when a mob had been about to execute her as a supposed traitor. "Lieutenant Kurinami and his fiance, Doctor Elaine Halversen, have been forced to flee into the wilds of the Georgia mountains, flee for their lives. I learned of this belatedly due to a pledge by Dodd that I would be informed, which precluded the Germans doing it themselves. At last, I was told of this turn of events by the Germans. There has been no word from Dodd. So, I'm the wrong man to ask."

The Chairman of the First City's brow knit into deep furrows. Michael's voice, so much like his own, cut through the silence. "Sir?"

"Yes, Mr. Rourke?"

"I share the feelings my father holds, but at the same time it would be worthwhile for this proposed embassy to the Second City to be comprised of, let's say, an impartial observer. Eden is due for a change of leadership. That seems inevitable. And when that time comes, were I to accompany this embassy, I could brief the new leadership concerning the embassy's results." Michael looked across the table.

John Rourke nodded, not approval but acceptance.

"You would be welcome, Michael," Otto Hammerschmidt declared.

"Yes," Han added; but his voice lacked emotion . . .

Sarah was waiting for him at the hospital, in the monorail level lobby when he arrived, wearing a dress of the Icelandic fashion, Empire waisted, her pregnancy so discreetly concealed beneath the long, bell-shaped skirt to be almost unnoticeable. John Rourke took her in his arms. "Any word?"

"Just that the operation was under way and we'd be notified. Annie and Paul are coming and should be here in a few minutes. Maria came by, then left to join Michael. She's in love with him."

"She's a nice girl." He cleared his throat. "Any word on Natalia's condition?"

"No change, I was told. That was a few hours ago. She eats poorly, cries. John?"

"What?"

"What are you going to do? Short of starting a harem, I mean?" She smiled when she said it and squeezed his hand as he sat down beside her.

Rolvaag undergoing major surgery, Natalia showing the classic symptoms of mental collapse, Kurinami and Halversen fleeing as fugitives from murder charges, Dodd no doubt pursuing them, his wife pregnant and his son going off to begin diplomatic negotiations with people who were spoken of as bloodthirsty barbarians. What was he going to do, he almost echoed aloud. The question was as pregnant as Sarah . . .

Mao stood on the platform and she watched him, as she had watched him when the self-proclaimed Russian soldier had been forced to hurtle himself into the pit.

There had been many smiles of approval, nods of gratitude and murmurs of support as he had entered the officers' recreation hall at the north corner of the main barracks, cheers as he had ascended the steps to the platform, his tonsured pate gleaming slightly with perspiration. He had always been uncomfortable as a public speaker, which somehow made him more effective, made him cling to the words which she gave him like a man thrown into the dog pit would cling to the leg of a guard.

Mao spoke and she didn't bother to listen, already knowing his words. Instead, she listened to the soft whispered words of the select group of assembled officers, both mercenary and enlisted, as they digested his edict. ". . . to the site where this battle supposedly took place. You will ascertain as best as available data suggests the extent and capabilities of the combatants. Colonel Wing. You will assume personal charge of the expeditionary force, and at the proper moment will dispatch riders to the City with your intelligence estimate while the main body of your force will pursue but not engage the assumedly weaker of the two forces. Is that understood?"

"Yes, Comrade Chairman. I will obey!"

Mao nodded his head, as though bowing, which of course he did to no one but her, and then only in the privacy of her apartments. "We must crush the weaker of these forces, then pursue the stronger! Victory!"

Mao raised his right fist and clenched it, the size it seemed, of a large hammer and as he crashed it down against the bare rostrum and it shook, a cheer thundered from the officers like a rumble from a rapidly advancing storm.

She was pleased . . .

John Rourke wore a white tropical weight dinner jacket, the kind of bow tie that was tied rather than clipped on (one could tell from the way the ends of the bow sagged slightly). He stood at the head of the stairs, his long legs spread slightly apart, as though he had stopped in mid-stride, as though nature had somehow freeze-framed him there. The photograph sent in the diplomatic pouch from Derzhinsky Square hadn't done him justice. He'd been exiting the plane, the collar of a heavy coat turned up against a strong wind that had tousled his hair, the collar obscuring much of his face. And the photo had only been in black and white.

Vladmir looked briefly into her eyes, then turned his head, craning his neck to stare toward the Miami Grande's main entrance where the American Case Officer Rourke, Vladmir had detemined, had to be killed tonight, stood.

The water couldn't be drunk since the revolutionary guard had blown up the American financed filtration plant (there was disease in the poorer parts of the capital but Vladmir had told her it was a small price for Central America's poor to pay for equality and justice). And so, on business tonight, Natalia Anastasia Tiemerovna, Captain, Committee for State Security of the Soviet, sipped at Chablis Blanc instead, watching him over the rim of her tulip shaped glass — it was the wrong shape for such a wine. John Rourke stepped onto the club's floor.

He moved with the grace of a black leopard, the surety of a stallion. She pushed a strand of her dyed blond hair back from her forehead with the back of her left hand, glancing at the time on the plain ladies Rolex on her wrist, mentally logging it for her report.

He walked toward the bar.

"That's him," Vladmir Karamotsav hissed across his vodka tumbler. Unlike her husband, she never drank hard liquor while working. She nodded almost imperceptibly that she knew that this man was Rourke, John Thomas, Case Officer, United States Central Intelligence Covert Operations Division, Central American

50

Special Action Group. "Go up to the bar and refill your glass. Get a closer look. See if you can spot his gun. That might come in handy. He's right-handed."

"All right, Vladmir," she whispered, not bothering to mention that had Vladmir read deeper into the file he would have learned that Rourke was, for all intents and purposes, ambidextrous. So was she.

The air was as heavy with smoke as it was with counterfeit American rock music as she drained off her glass and stood, catching up the skirt of her white ankle length gown and starting toward the bar where the American leaned, at once casual yet somehow seeming uncomfortable.

She knew his name, assumed his politics, knew why the CIA had sent him, but found herself wondering what he was really like.

Natalia reached the bar.

"Si—another Chablis Blanc, please. It was house brand I think." The bartender—a greasy looking man in a white bolero length jacket—nodded and smiled at her as he took the glass, his hand intentionally touching hers for an instant. She dismissed it, like accidentally touching a dirty doorknob. She glanced to her left, looking at this John Rourke. His forehead was high, but naturally so, his dark brown hair thick, healthy looking. As if he felt her watching him, he inclined his head toward her and before she averted her eyes, she saw his. They were brown, filled with steadiness and a hint of melancholy and she felt a nervous feeling suddenly deep in the pit of her stomach.

He was either very good at concealing a weapon—better than she would have thought he should be—or unarmed. She determined that as her eyes crossed over his body plane when the bartender brought her the glass of wine. There was no hint of a telltale bulge under his jacket. Perhaps an ankle holster, the trouser legs wide enough for one if it were worn properly. "Put the wine on our bill—over there," she told the bartender, then ignored him and walked back from the bar. Vladmir stood but didn't get her chair. She sat down, raising her glass to her lips, saying over it, "Either he isn't armed at all or he's better than anyone I've seen at concealing. He could have an ankle holster, but I didn't see anything to indicate he did."

"What did his file say?"

"He carries a .45 automatic, a Colt, sometimes two of them."

"Any mention of a backup gun?"

"He carries a knife. An A.G. Russell Sting, it said, or sometimes a big Gerber."

"Then we'll take him easily enough. You can see him better. Who's he talking to?"

She lit a cigarette and looked across the flame of the lighter toward the bar. John Rourke was speaking with a Latin wearing a white dinner jacket, the Latin smoking a cigarette, holding it carelessly in his right hand, gesturing with it as he spoke. His name was Armando Fernandez-Salizar and he was head of the pro-American government's counter-terrorist unit, his identity a closely guarded state secret. Fernandez-Salizar must have been in a back room, because she had not seen him at the bar before this instant. Fernandez-Salizar did not know that his identity was known.

"What is he doing, Natalia? I don't want to—"

"You're in luck tonight, Vladmir. Fernandez-Salizar is standing at the bar with him. You can get the both—wait—"

"What?"

The American, Rourke, and Fernandez-Salizar were walking around the end of the bar, a door opening quickly, both of them disappearing through the doorway. "They're leaving—it looked like a back room."

"Merde!" Vladmir hissed. Vladmir stood up, patting his pockets vigorously. Then, in a voice calculated to be heard over the loudness of the Latinized Rock, said, "I left that other pack of cigarettes in the car, sweetheart. Be back in a flash."

She smiled, Vladmir leaving the room, heading toward the steps and the entrance.

Natalia took her beaded bag from the table beside her cigarettes and lighter, using the mirror in the purse's flap to look toward the door beside the bar. It remained closed.

She picked up her cigarettes and her lighter, starting to put them away. " . . . cigarettes in the car . . ." meant that he was going to get the rest of the men. ". . . sweetheart" meant that she should follow the subject, in this case subjects, Rourke and Fernandez-Salizar. ". . . flash" meant they'd hit in ten minutes. She had already ticked off sixty seconds mentally and glanced at her watch. At eleven fourteen, Vladmir's people would come in, some through the main entrance and some through whatever back door presented itself. There would be a bloodbath unless she could get Rourke and Fernandez-Salizar herself and defuse Vladmir's operation.

Natalia stood up, tugging at her dress, letting it settle, turning her head toward the doorway through which Rourke and Fernandez-Salizar had disappeared.

She started toward the doorway, catching a glimpse of the bartender moving too quickly, his right hand snaking under the white jacket. "Senorita—it is prohibited!"

She stopped less than a yard from the door. She looked at him. He came under the bar's drop leaf, his hand still under his jacket. "It's all right. I'm expected," she told him.

"Senorita—is prohibited."

She shrugged her shoulders a little, making her cleavage deepen, his eyes widening, her left hand brushing against the left side of his torso. The gun she'd thought she'd spotted earlier was there. She started past him, stopped.

"Senorita—"

She had her dress up over her left knee, her right hand to the garter sheath and the Bali-Song pressured against the inside of her left thigh. Her fingers closed over it as she let the skirt fall and turned toward him quickly, "Pero, senor—es muy importante—"

The click-click-click sound she had heard so many times, the sudden hardness in the eyes, the hand sweeping the gun out, but not in time, the Bali-Song's blade tip gouging into the neck and ripping as she stepped back quickly so the arterial blood wouldn't ruin her dress, the body lurching toward her, collapsing to the knees, the gun—a Walther P-38—falling from limpening fingers. She reached down quickly and in one fluid motion, had the gun in her tiny left fist, the Bali-Song's blade wiped clean against the dying man's coat sleeve and was moving toward the door. Click-click-click. She dropped the Bali-Song down her cleavage, her purse under her left upper arm, her left hand shifting the 9mm to her right, then sweeping across the slide. She had never trusted loaded chamber indicators or the fact that a double action pistol with a state-of-the-art safety system would be carried chamber loaded. As the slide snapped back, she heard the ejected cartridge hit the end of the bar. She heard a woman scream, then a man scream. The rock music was still playing annoyingly loudly.

The doorknob turned under her hand, but only enough to tell her it was locked.

Natalia stepped back, levelling the P-38 at the lockplate on the side nearest the jamb, firing twice in rapid succession. She would have five or six rounds left, depending. She wheeled half right, her left hand bunching her dress up to her thighs as her left leg snapped up and out, the sole of her left foot hitting the lockplate, the door slamming open inward.

She ran through the doorway, seeing Fernandez-Salizar already turning around, another man wearing a black business suit and holding a riot shotgun wheeling toward her. There was no sign of John Rourke. Natalia pulled the Walther's trigger, then again, blood flowering at the center of the shotgunner's forehead and near his adam's apple just over his shirt collar, the body rocking away as she wheeled toward Fernandez-Salizar. He was drawing a revolver. Her first bullet went through his right wrist and he shrieked with pain, falling back. But he still tried making his hand work enough to get the gun from under the left side of his coat, his formal shirt front splotching with blood from the first bullet's secondary wound. Her second bullet went into his chest properly this time and, as he fell, she fired a third shot through his left eye. It was important that he be dead.

The Walther's slide was locked open. There had only been seven rounds.

The shotgun was too obvious.

Natalia let the P-38 drop to the floor.

She tore Fernandez-Salizar's hand away from the butt of the revolver and pulled it the rest of the way from the shoulder holster (it was a four-inch nickel Colt Python, flashy, big and macho looking just as she had expected). Her right hand was sticky with blood from the grips. There was no time to wipe it off. There was no time to check the load.

As the first man from the Miami Grande bar came through the door, a Browning High Power in both hands like some cop on American television, she fired a double tap just in case the first chamber had been left empty, an old trick some police and security people who still clung to revolvers used in case their gun was taken away and turned against them.

But both chambers were charged and his body slammed back through the doorway.

Where was the American, Rourke?

Natalaia Timerovna wheeled away from the doorway back into the bar, glancing at her watch. Seven minutes before Vladmir would send in his people with the submachineguns. Perhaps the gunfire would have alerted him that it wasn't necessary? But that didn't stop the kinds of men he used. Tell them to kill and they smiled. "Sometimes, to advance the cause, Natalia darling, men like these can be useful," he had told her more than once.

There was another doorway and the .357 Magnum with four shots remaining still in her right hand, she opened the door, a narrow, bare yellow-bulb-lit corridor beyond. Her purse in her left hand, her fingertips hitching up her dress so she could move quickly, Natalia ran the length of the corridor, eyes flickering side-to-side toward the doorways she passed. Performers dressing rooms perhaps. She could smell makeup.

At the far end of the corridor was a door, she opened it and stepped back quickly, in case the American was waiting in the alley beyond.

There was no gunfire and she stepped quickly through the shaft of yellow light and onto a small landing, flattening herself against the wall just beyond the door. She might be ruining her dress.

She saw no one in the alley, then heard gunfire from the end of the alley. Pistol caliber automatic weapons. The heavier thudding of a .45 automatic.

Natalia started down the steps to the alley floor. She saw a flash of white moving toward her. The American in his white dinner jacket?

Natalia stepped back into the shadows.

Two of the thugs her husband hired were chasing after

him. The American threw himself down behind a rank of trash cans as the alley wall exploded under submachinegun-fire impact. He rolled from cover and fired, a tongue of orange flame licking into the night, then another and another, one of the submachinegunners down.

The second man charged toward him and the American, Rourke, was on his feet, the submachinegunner firing, Rourke firing, the second man going down.

Rourke started running, coming toward her now, going for the fence that blocked her end of the alley.

Natalia put her purse under her left arm, raising the Python in both hands, tracking him as he ran until the range would make a miss impossible.

He was coming into the cone of the alley light.

He looked toward the doorway.

Natalia saw his face.

She lowered the revolver.

"Thanks!" He ran past her, to the fence, vaulting over it as if it were only eight inches tall rather than eight feet. He was gone.

"Thanks" he had said, this John Rourke . . . Natalia sat up, the hospital gown soaked with sweat. She brought her hands to her eyes, felt the tears streaming down her cheeks.

"John!" Her own voice sounded to her like a muffled scream.

The first time she had seen John Rourke, her life had forever changed. The questions that had remained unspoken inside her about Vladmir and what he told her was right and good to do had become more nagging.

She had always thought that stories of love at first sight were only for naive girls. And then she had learned that she was one.

Natalia Anastasia Timerovna closed her eyes, wanting to see John's face again in her self-imposed darkness.

But she could only see Vladmir's face, the look of horror in his eyes, the horror of recognizing the moment of his own death as her arms had arced John's massive knife toward his throat and steel first touched flesh and blood sprayed on her hands and face.

Natalia opened her eyes, realizing she was gasping for breath. She could still see Vladmir's face.

CHAPTER SEVEN

Hans Weil's eyes scanned the ground as they had with each step he had taken for hours and, at last, beneath the shelter of a scrub pine, where the drifting snow had not reached, he saw a partial footprint, the portion of the sole impression matching perfectly to the design of Eden Project issue boots. "Horst! Here!" Weil shouted, dropping to his knees to examine more carefully the boot's print in the snow.

"Hans?"

"Here!" Was it the man, Kurinami, or the black woman, Halversen? Japanese were smaller statured than western men and the footsize would be correspondingly smaller, he knew. He couldn't tell to which of the two they hunted the footprint belonged.

"What is this?"

"Horst—look here. A footprint. Dodd was right. They travel toward the Herr Doctor Rourke's Retreat."

"You had better call Dodd on the radio, I think," Horst nodded gravely, pulling away his snow mask and tugging his goggles down to where they hung loosely around his neck.

"Yes." Weil took the radio from the carrier on his vest. He telescoped the flexible antenna and pointed it southward, depressing the push to talk button under his gloved thumb. "Arrow Three to Archer. Arrow Three calling Archer. Come in, Archer." He waited. There was only static. "This is Arrow Three calling Archer. Do you read me? Over."

Horst started to speak, then the radio crackled and he heard Dodd's voice. "Arrow Three, this is Archer. Reading you loud and clear. Over."

"Archer. Have located sign of prey near designated area. All is confirmed. Over."

"Arrow Three. Say again. Over."

"Archer. Have located some sign of prey. Indicates destination is designated area. All is confirmed as per your briefing. Over."

"Arrow Three. Contact Arrow One, Arrow Two and Arrow Four. The word is Pearl. I say again, Pearl. Understood? Over."

"The word is Pearl. Understood. Arrow Three Over."

"Archer Out."

"Arrow Three Out." And Weil switched frequencies, setting to the common frequency shared with Arrow One, Two and Four. He studied his watch. In ten minutes it would be time for the regular call up.

"So we go to this Retreat, then?"

"Yes. And we wait for Kurinami and Halversen. They have to come out sometime."

Horst laughed. "The Herr Doctor and his family— they stayed inside for five hundred years."

Weil saw nothing funny in it at all and he was very cold . . .

Annie Rourke finished drying her hair and started brushing it. In the old movies on videotape that her father kept at The Retreat, she would sometimes see women with such impossibly short haircuts. It would have to be easier to wash and care for, of course, but still, she thought—"What do you think about Michael and this deal with the Second City?" Paul called from the bathroom. She still liked watching him shave and as she looked into the vanity mirror, she could just see his image in the bathroom mirror, half his face still white and foamy with lather.

"I don't know. It scares me. Those people are crazy, from what I hear. I'd like to say they'd listen to reason, but—"

"No vibes on it?"

She laughed. "No vibes." Her "psychic abilities," if that was what they were properly called, were telling her nothing—yet. But she had never really considered that pre-cognition was something which really worked at all. She had her "flashes" while the event was actually transpiring, not before. If she ever started to see the future, she wondered if she would be able to handle it without losing her sanity. Just the thought of it made her shiver as she ran the brush through her waist length brown hair. Her father had always told her it was "honey blond" and that there were threads of gold in her hair, but to her it had always just been brown. Natalia's hair—that was a different story, so dark a brown that it was almost a true black, such a lustrous—

"You sure you wanna go back to Georgia with us?"

"Akiro and Elaine are my friends, too. Mom'll be all right here. And Maria's staying when Michael leaves. Once Natalia's out of the hospital, they can all keep each other company. We shouldn't be long anyway. I'm sure Commander Dodd is just a screw up and doesn't have any insidious purposes or anything like that—don't you think, Paul?"

"I don't know what to think," he said, coming out the bathroom. He wasn't wearing anything but the bathrobe she had made for him. And his almost black, thinning hair was still wet from the shower and the wetness made his head look shiny where there wasn't any hair. She thought it looked sexy but never mentioned it because he was self-conscious about his thinning hair

61

and she was self-conscious about hurting his feelings. There was a tiny fleck of white soap on his neck. He usually shaved before he showered, but had told her he was so tired from the ordeal of the hospital that if he didn't run through the shower first he'd fall asleep while he shaved. And they had to get back to be with her father and mother when the operation on Bjorn Rolvaag was completed so there wasn't any time to sleep.

She hadn't like the hospital either. She stood up and walked over to him, with her finger wiping the shaving cream off his neck. "Miss something?"

"Hmm —" he leaned over her and took her in his arms and kissed her hard on the mouth. She rubbed the shaving cream off her finger and onto his nose, escaping his hands as they closed around her. "I'll get pimples," he laughed.

She only smiled.

Paul was fully dressed before she had her underwear on but she tried to hurry, getting into one of the Chinese dresses with the slit along the left thigh and getting Paul to zip it up the back for her. She could have zipped it herself but it was more fun having him fumble with the little hook and eye at the collar. They weren't in that much of a hurry, the laser surgery scheduled to take at least another hour.

They left their apartment in the Government building and took the monorail back to the hospital, Paul sitting beside her and holding both her hands in one of his and telling her not to worry, that Rolvaag would be fine. She didn't worry, somehow feeling that he would.

She had pondered why, when her father had been shot by the Russians in their underwater complex while he'd been trying to rescue Natalia, and was near death — why she hadn't felt the danger reaching out to her, felt that he was in trouble. And she reasoned that perhaps she had felt it and been unable to sort out her feelings, in so

62

much danger herself then. Or was it that she hadn't listened to her feelings because they frightened her and on one level of her consciousness she had dismissed them?

She would never understand this "gift" as those who didn't have it called it. But that it was more a curse seemed obvious. By the time she really felt anything about his plight, he had been on his way back to Mid-Wake for repairs to his surgery after the fight to the death with Karamatsov. And then too, she had just felt it that he would be all right. Like she felt now about Bjorn Rolvaag. She made a mental note to go to the veterinary hospital and play with his dog for him before she left with Paul. Hrothgar would be lonely without his master.

As the monorail neared the hospital, other feelings took hold of her. For Natalia. She sensed confusion, sorrow, despair. If she hadn't known better, she would have worried that Natalia wanted to take her own life. "Hold my hands tighter, Paul," she implored . . .

Natalia Anastasia Tiemerovna sat cross-legged, her black canvas bag — it could be used as a purse or a small day pack — on the hospital bed before her.

When the plastic razor blade had been crafted for her to be hidden in her boot, she had ordered a second one, hidden this inside her purse.

She held the razor blade over her left wrist and stared at her vein.

There was really no sense in living. If she died, John would grieve, remember her, but— With the baby coming, the grief he felt for her death would be washed away by joy, his joy and Sarah's.

Living only caused more grief for John. It was important to understand, despite what John espoused, that some situations were indeed hopeless, that sometimes there wasn't any choice left but giving up.

She lay the razor blade against her skin. It felt warm to the touch, the warmth of her own hand from having held it for the last hour.

Natalia began humming a tune. She couldn't remember its name. So she kept humming it over and over again, trying to remember, her eyes fixed on the razor blade where it touched her flesh. One fast movement and a few brief moments of pain and then a tired feeling and a warm sleep where there would be no dreams of loving John or killing Vladmir and it would all be ended. She would miss dreaming about John.

She couldn't name the melody, but it was very sad and just hearing her own voice cooing it brought a melancholy feeling over her that hadn't been there, the sadness replacing the calm, the razor blade falling from her fingers as tears welled up in her eyes and she felt them roll down her cheeks, her tears seeming to her like acid burning her eyes and her flesh and her soul.

CHAPTER EIGHT

Michael Rourke, his gear packed and sent off with Han and Otto to the waiting German helicopter, stepped from the monorail, Maria Leuden beside him. Maria looked beautiful, he thought, wearing one of the Chinese style dresses they called a chong san. Michael Rourke was in full battle gear, his handmade double shoulder rig with the twin Berettas, the knife made for him by old Jon the Icelandic bladesmith, the four-inch Smith 629 in the holster at his hip.

"You look like you are on your way to a war, not a peace mission," she said quietly, looking up at him, her gray-green eyes half shadowed by her lids, her eyelashes seeming impossibly long at the angle, like a long ago memory of a butterfly folding its wings.

"Peace through superior firepower," Michael grinned, letting Maria walk ahead of him through the pneumatic doors into the hospital lobby. His father, the battered old brown leather bomber jacket wide open (his guns would be under it), paced the floor, his mother standing beside the machine which dispensed hot Chinese tea in various flavors. Sometimes Michael found himself longing for the scenes he vaguely remembered from his youth — soft drink machines everywhere and real Coca-Cola that wasn't five centuries old like the few bottles left at The Retreat.

"Mom. Dad," he began, his father ceasing to pace in mid-stride, turning toward them, Maria moving ahead slightly, his father embracing her like a daughter (would he — Michael — ask Maria to be his wife? he wondered). His mother set down the two red plastic cups of tea on the small table beside the long couch beside which she stood, then embraced Maria in turn.

"Son," John Rourke said, extending his right hand. Michael took it, held it a moment. He sensed his father's awkwardness as much as he sensed his own, smiled, released his father's hand, his father's eyes smiling. His mother put her arms around his neck and kissed him lightly on the lips, then held him close to her for a moment. Biologically, as opposed to chronologically, Sarah Rourke was barely old enough to be an older sister and he and his father, he was reminded once again, looked enough alike to be twin brothers. "Any word on Bjorn, yet?" Michael asked.

"Nothing," his mother told them. "But I suppose no news is probably good news in this case. Sit down. Would you like some tea?"

"I can get it, Frau Rourke," Maria Leuden volunteered, drifting off toward the dispenser.

"How about Natalia?" Michael asked, taking a seat opposite his father and mother as they sat.

His father just shook his head.

"Nothing has changed. She's resting," Sarah Rourke told them. "I think she's just really tired. And, God help her, what she did — it's a miracle Natalia hasn't lost her sanity. All of us need a rest, and she needs it more than any of us. The tension — of all this," Sarah Rourke concluded, taking a sip of her tea, setting it down, folding her hands in her lap then with an air of helplessness. With her hands in her lap that way, the baby seemed suddenly noticeable. As a grown man, it was hard to accept the fact that he would soon have a new brother or sister. Doctor Munchen, or for that matter the medical wizards of Mid-Wake, could have determined the sex of the child or even altered it to suit the desired sex with relative ease. Eye color, hair color, all could have been altered. But Sarah Rourke had insisted that she wanted to find out the old fashioned way.

Michael Rourke secretly felt that his mother and father's decision was probably best, but had said nothing. It was not his affair to say.

"Look — ahh —" As Maria handed him one of the red plastic cups of tea, he started to suggest that he and Maria could go up and visit Natalia, but he heard Annie's voice behind them.

"Any word?"

"Nothing," Michael called back to her without looking around.

Annie made the rounds of hugs and kisses, Paul a handshake here and there.

Michael Rourke looked at his watch. There was nothing to do but wait, he supposed . . .

The coordinates from the Eden computer pinpointed the location of Doctor Rourke's mountain retreat to within a hundred yards. There was no mistaking the location from binocular range, Weil thought.

A pinnacle of granite extending upward above the surrounding peaks. But even at highest magnification, there was no hint of an entrance.

Horst too was studying The Retreat, Weil not shifting his gauge but listening as Horst spoke. "As soon as the other teams are here, we will go up there. We will find the way inside. This Herr Doctor Rourke is so very clever, but we shall see how clever, I think."

Weil let him talk. Horst had always displayed a propensity for talking before thinking, in the old days at the beer sessions after the party meetings, back at the youth rallies. Some things never changed.

Weil stamped his feet against the cold, the binoculars moving slowly over what Dodd called Rourke's Mountain . . .

The pilot of the helicopter gunship announced, "Comrade Colonel. We are past the coordinates. You requested to be notified."

"Thank you," Antonovitch said perfunctorily. He switched on his headset. "Antonovitch to ground control. Connect me with Major Prokopiev immediately."

There was the standard response accorded, then a pause he measured as barely exceeding thirty seconds. Prokopiev's voice came through his headset. "Comrade Colonel. This is Prokopiev. I await your instructions. Over."

Antonovitch smiled. The man he had chosen to head up the newly reorganized Elite Corps was efficient. Whether or not he would prove to be too efficient remained to be seen. "Prokopiev. Plan Omega is activated. Necessary data will be transmitted following. Good luck, Comrade. Antonovitch out." He switched off, then changed to intraship. "Signalman. Transmit the data."

"Yes, Comrade Colonel."

He would keep his colonel's insignia for a while longer, despite the Principal Secretary calling him Marshal. He would wait and he would see . . .

Akiro Kurinami entered the reserve arms locker. Rourke's personal weapons were encased in glass on the wall of the Great Room and he would no more think of touching one of these without permission than touching another man's wife. But the reserve arms locker was another matter.

Sleep would not come to him. He envied Elaine, soundly asleep on the guest room bed. And she looked beautiful in the borrowed nightgown. He imagined it was the property of Rourke's daughter, Annie, who seemed the frilly type despite her prowess with weapons and her cold logic.

The reserve arms locker was a vault within the vault that formed The Retreat itself.

He recognized some of the long guns: collapsible stock Colt AR-15s, the civilian semi-auto versions of the M-16 variant known as the XM-77, the barrel only slightly longer; Steyr-Mannlicher SSG sniper rifles; there were also a dozen M-16s. Rourke had told him once that before the Night of The War he had not bothered with automatic weapons. The licensing provisions were intrusive of privacy, the licensing fees exorbitant and the cost of the weapons themselves astronomical. And, for someone operating independently of an armed force and the sources of supply it would provide, automatic weapons invited ammunition over-expenditure. But since the Night of The War, Rourke had, on several occasions, "liberated" (as he put it) the selective fire versions of the Colt rifle. And, as Kurinami's eyes traveled across the olive drab metal boxes stacked along the floor beneath the rifle rack, ammunition supply was apparently no longer a potential problem. The Germans, of course. Rourke had gotten them to fabricate for him all the ammunition he needed in the calibers he favored and hence required.

Twenty and thirty round magazines were crated beside the ammunition. He took six of these latter and one of the metal boxes of 5.56mm Ball and one of the M-16s from the rack, stacking the items neatly beside the door.

There were various handguns, a blued version of the little Detonics .45s Rourke habitually carried, a half dozen of the Beretta 92F military 9mm Parabellums.

He took one off the rack, the oil heavy on it as it had been on the M-16 when he'd touched it. The gun was marked as made in Italy, meaning it was from one of the early runs before production was shifted to the United States. He took several spare fifteen round magazines and two of the twenty-round magazines, setting gun and magazines beside the already stacked weapons. He set about finding 9mm Parabellum ammunition. 115-grain jacketed hollow points. This would, of course, duplicate the Federal cartridge loads, Rourke a man of definite tastes. He set the ammunition on the floor.

A blade. Somehow, a blade was what he would take the greatest comfort from. And he found one. Knives marked Gerber and Cold Steel were suspended against a pegboard wall inset. He took down one in the classic conformation of a coffin-handled Bowie fighter. The handle was of some sort of black checkered rubber-like substance, the fittings brass, the steel gleamingly bright. It was marked "Trail Master."

Rourke had explained to him once that each weapon he inventoried was logged in the P.C. on disc with pertinent information.

Kurinami found a sheath that seemed right—it was black leather—then in several trips took his borrowed weapons from the arms locker back into the Great Room.

He secured the arms locker, washed the oil off his hands in the kitchen sink—he would worry about the oil on the kitchen counter later—and dried them.

Kurinami went to the computer, several transparent lid plastic boxes beside it, each loaded with discs. He began to search through these, finding the disc marked, "File Master," then inserting it into the drive and punching it up. File Master was a key to the contents of the discs and he found the one he wanted: "Weapons Data." He changed discs and worked through the formatted file list, finding the right file, punching it up.

The Beretta: it had been throated and checked with hollow points and shot to point of aim. The M-16, like the Beretta listed by several number, was listed as functionally reliable but not the most accurate of the several M-16s logged. The Trail Master Bowie: A special type of high carbon steel, it was not stainless but, according to Rourke's remarks, was admirably strong and sharp.

Kurinami shut off the P.C. and replaced the discs in the proper slots in the boxes.

He was wide awake still. He stood up, walked back to the kitchen counter and set about finding what he needed to clean the guns.

Dodd wanted him dead. That was obvious. Why? And as he began to field strip the Beretta, he remembered the face of one of the men who had tortured him, kidnapped Elaine, would have killed them both.

It was a face he had never seen before, neither among the Eden Project survivors nor among the German garrison.

But whose face was it?

CHAPTER NINE

John Rourke looked down on Rolvaag's face. "Old friend. I wish you could understand me."

Annie leaned over the Icelandic policeman as his eyelids fluttered, then opened. She seemed to have a natural gift for Icelandic or perhaps just a gift for speaking with Rolvaag and her voice sounded almost as if she were singing as she spoke, Rolvaag's face still weary but a momentary brightness in his eyes, a slurred word of recognition, then a look of peace on his face as he closed his eyes again when Annie kissed him on the forehead.

"He knows," Annie said, looking up, Paul folding her into his arms. "That he'll be all right now. He knows." And her eyes danced for a moment. "And I told him Hrothgar's all right, too."

John Rourke had all the principals together in one room and he used the moment. "Paul and Annie and I'll go to Georgia and see about clearing up this business with Kurinami and Elaine Halverson. Michael—don't take this mission to the Second City too lightly. And remember that Han, despite the fact he's your friend, as you told me yourself, owes the death of his family to raiders from the Second City. Men driven by revenge can view the world a little differently, as you well know. Remember the first thing you said to me when we met again after Karamatsov was killed?"

"I said that you cheated me of doing it myself. But Natalia really did it," Michael Rourke said quietly. "And

I told her that I had wanted Karamatsov's death more than I wanted anything and now I'd never have it and maybe I should thank her."

"Remember your own emotions this trip when you try to interpret Han's emotions, then," John Rourke told his son, then to all of them, "Paul and Annie and I should be back in a few days. All of us have to be concerned with getting Natalia well, maybe getting her back to Iceland. She might be happier there and she'd be farther away from her memories there."

"You should spend some time with her before you go, John," Sarah announced.

"Momma's right," Annie whispered.

"I know your mother's right. And I'm going to see her. Paul? Come, too?"

"Of course," the younger man nodded.

John Rourke said nothing, but embraced his son tightly for a moment, then left the room, Paul after him . . .

"I'm fine. Really I am. I mean, the doctors are right. I should relax a little. Maybe focus my energies on something else. I'm really just fine," Natalia smiled, her eyes sparkling—but perhaps she had only just been crying, Paul Rubenstein thought. He stood a bit back from the two of them, watching. They were made for each other, Natalia Tiemerovna and John Rourke. He had said it often in the pages of the journal he kept with intermittent but satisfactory regularity even since the Night of The War. He was reminded of the somewhat trite sounding expression "star-crossed lovers," but indeed they were that.

John held her hands in his. "Are you sure you're feeling better?"

"You know Russians—depression comes and goes

73

with us. I'm fine. I'd be a liar if I said everything was perfect and I was happy, but I'm all right, John. You take care of this thing with that crazy man Dodd accusing Akiro and Elaine. I only wish the doctors would release me so I could go too. But they want me here for another few days. I'll be out and around and Sarah and Maria and I can see everything there is to see in the First City. You know the last time I shopped? Five hundred years ago! And I've got all the credit I want since these people insisted on rewarding us for stopping that train with the missiles. So see? What more could a woman ask? Unlimited funds, two friends to chatter with and a whole city to explore and buy out," she laughed, but the laughter didn't sound quite right to him. "I want some of those dresses like Annie's been wearing. And, you know, they even sell silk underwear here! and I love silk underwear. So, I'll be fine. Now, both of you, kiss me. None of this peck on the cheek kissing, either, Paul," and Natalia held out her arms to him.

Paul Rubenstein was suddenly afraid for her, and as he embraced her and softly kissed her lips he felt a cold shiver deep within.

He hugged her, stepped back, John leaning over the bed, drawing her close to him, holding her for a long time. "And don't you dare say it, John," she smiled. And then John Rourke kissed her and Paul Rubenstein looked away . . .

John Rourke, a light blue snap front cowboy shirt half out of his Levis, slung the double Alessi shoulder rig across his back, the twin stainless Detonics .45 Combat Masters chamber loaded and secured. He stuffed the shirttails the rest of the way down, beginning to thread his belt, the black leather sheath for the Crain Life Support System X going on his left side, then the Sparks

Six-Pak loaded with six-round Detonics magazines. He threaded the belt the rest of the way and cinched it closed.

The A.G. Russell Sting IA black chrome. He secured the knife in its spring clip sheath near the small of his back inside the waistband of his jeans.

His gunbelt with the Metalifed and Mag-na-Ported Colt Python six-inch. He secured it just below his trouser belt, the sheath for the Crain knife going over it.

Rourke picked up the twelve-inch bladed knife, turning it in his hand. With this knife, Natalia had ended the life of Vladmir Karamatsov. Although weapons were only instruments, he wondered if it better belonged in a museum for veneration by those who would no longer have to live in fear of the madman. But he sheathed it, because there were other evils in the world.

Rourke took up his musette bag, slinging it cross body from right shoulder to left hip, then skinned into the battered brown leather bomber jacket. He patted the pockets. His immediate supply of cigars, his sunglasses, his gloves.

Rourke caught up the M-16 and the second bag, this filled with magazines for the assault rifle.

Like the knife and his other weapons, he knew that he would have a use for it. He gave a last glance at the empty apartment — Sarah would be waiting by the tunnel leading out of the city — and started for the doorway . . .

The German helicopter's rotor blades turned more rapidly as John Rourke took Sarah Rourke into his arms.

"I'll take care of Natalia," she told him.

"Take care of yourself and the baby — for me," and he kissed her hard on the mouth, holding her close.

Over the whoosh of the rotor blades, he could hear Paul calling, "Everything's aboard, John!"

Rourke looked at Sarah. Her gray-green eyes. Her auburn hair. Her smile. "I really love you," he said quietly, kissed her again — quickly — then caught up his rifle and the Lowe pack and broke into a run for the chopper, keeping his head low as he crossed beneath the whirring blades.

He tossed the Lowe pack through the doorway, then handed up his M-16, Annie taking it.

As he stepped aboard, he looked back. Her left hand clutched gently at her abdomen and the life there, and her right hand waved toward him.

John Rourke blew her a kiss, then slid the door home. "All secure, pilot!"

Rourke eased back into one of the bench seats. There would be time enough to go forward and assume his duties as co-pilot.

For now, as the helicopter — Germans called them machines which screwed themselves into the air — lifted off, snow swirling cyclonically in its wake, he held his daughter's hand and watched the rapidly vanishing figure of his wife.

Sarah still waved.

CHAPTER TEN

Vassily Mikhailovitch Prokopiev, Major, Commanding, Elite Corps, Committee For State Security of The Soviet, stepped to the open hatchway, the wind tearing at him, the jump light flashing to green. Prokopiev tapped the senior sergeant on the shoulder, the senior sergeant signalling the first man to jump. No static lines, high altitude, low-opening. The light flickered amber, then green again, the next man jumping at the senior sergeant's signal, the flicker of the light again, then the green, the next man out, man after man, full battle gear in place. Prokopiev took his eye off the doorway and looked across the fuselage through the transparent panel in the starboard side door, the other two high altitude capable silenced gunships disgorging their jumpers, the cargo chutes (these would open electronically when altimeter readings were proper).

Prokopiev looked back to the jumpers on his own craft. One more, then the senior sergeant, then himself, the two lieutenants under him assigned one each to the jumpers with the other two gunships. He tugged at his equipment for the last time, all secure.

The senior sergeant, Piotr Yaroslav, glanced at him once, then jumped, Prokopiev stepping into the doorway, watching below as Yaroslav's image vanished into the darkness. Yaroslav — it was likely one of those names assumed during the violent days immediately before the

77

1917 Revolution, then merely passed on.

Green light.

Prokopiev jumped, somewhere to the north in the darkness surrounding him, the Second Chinese City waiting . . .

"Herr Doctor?"

John Rourke took his eyes from the control panel he had been studying, Adolph Lintz, the young German lieutenant whose ship the J7-V was, returning to the cockpit.

"I am able to relieve you now, Herr Doctor. Thank you. It is a long flight." Lintz was tall, thin in the extreme, his face beneath the close cropped blond hair cheerful, however bony.

"But a good rest awaits you at the German facility outside Eden Base," Rourke smiled, the officer seating himself at the pilot's controls. "Somehow, that doesn't seem to cheer you, Lieutenant."

The young German laughed as he took the yoke and Rourke released simultaneously. "My wife, Olga, is in New Germany—Argentina as you would call it, Herr Doctor. I have not seen her for three months."

"Men have survived longer periods than that," Rourke smiled again, unstrapping, rising from the co-pilot's seat. "But I hope you get to see her soon."

"She is very pretty."

"I noticed the picture," and Rourke gestured toward the photograph wedged between the mounting frame and the landing gear control panel. She was blonde, trim waisted and almost classically large bosomed—and undoubtedly much more pleasant to hold on a cold night than the controls of a J7-V V-Stol fighter bomber.

"Then you know what I mean. It will be good to rest at our facility near Eden Base. But—" And he exhaled long and softly. "It is not the same as being with my Olga."

"Here." And John Rourke took his wallet from his jacket where he'd taken to carrying it since The Awakening. Wrapped inside a waterproof plastic bag, he opened the bag, then extracted one of the laminated photographs from inside. "Her name is Sarah." He extended the picture in his hand and Lieutenant Lintz took it.

"She is so pretty, your wife. Very beautiful. You are having a baby, I understand?"

"Sarah is, actually," Rourke nodded. The young fellow was apparently starved for conversation, or naturally curious, or perhaps both. Rourke took back the photograph of his wife, returning it to his wallet, returning the wallet to the bag and then to his pocket as he continued. "She's through the first trimester."

"You must be excited. Olga and I — we want children. If I speak out of turn, Herr Doctor Rourke, please tell me to be quiet. But — your daughter — in there —" And Lintz gestured with a cock of the head toward the compartment just aft of the cockpit.

"She's twenty-eight."

"I have heard the story — I know I am rude —"

Rourke sat back down and buckled in. There was time. "Briefly, after we took the cryogenic sleep as the Great Conflagration began, I awoke early, then awakened my son, Michael, and my daughter, Annie. I stayed with them for five years and returned to the Sleep when I thought they were adequately prepared to function together on their own. I continued in the cryogenic sleep until Annie was nearing the end of her twenty-seventh year. The children had aged to adulthood, while I only aged five years and my wife, Sarah, aged virtually not at all. The same held true or the man who's now her husband, Paul Rubenstein, and, of course, Major Tiemerovna."

"Ahh — she is pretty. Major Tiemerovna. I saw her.

She has a face a man would die for, I think."

"Yes," John Rourke almost whispered . . .

Weil felt suddenly oppressively warm and began removing his parka. In the night, outside, it had been bone-chillingly cold, the temperatures throughout the period of the last several days dropping almost imperceptibly at first, but now more than a man could bear at night. Would they continue to drop? He longed for the warmth of his native New Germany. But the spirit of the Reich had to be served, and participating in this Dodd's conspiracy was the only available means by which this end could be accomplished. If the Japanese officer and the black woman with him had been unable to reach Herr Rourke's mountain retreat there would have been no need to worry over them. Without one of the hermetically sealed tents, they would have died, regardless of whatever survival training they had been given. Weil sat at the table now, the men from the other teams idling away the night playing cards, reading. Only Horst was still out in it, still scanning the mountain with his vision intensification binoculars, huddled as close as he could get to the field heater, searching for some secret and penetrable entrance into Rourke's Mountain.

Failing that Horst found such an entrance, there was the other alternative. Weil glanced toward the explosives stacked in the far corner of the tent. He lit a cigarette . . .

John Rourke saw to his gear, the Lowe Alpine Systems Loco Pack secure, his leather jacket inside. Snowshoes or cross country skis might have been useful, he thought, considering the weather. He pulled on the heavy gray woolen sweater, glancing at the Rolex on his left wrist. Nearly time. "Paul?"

"All set, John," the younger man called back, kneeling, helping Annie with her boots.

Rourke found himself watching his daughter intently. It was odd seeing her in pants, but even with her decidedly feminine tastes she hadn't said a word when they had discussed the return to Georgia and he — John Rourke — had cited German meteorological reports. The pre-dawn low here was anticipated to reach minus twenty degrees, the windchill factor creating the effect of minus fifty degrees Fahrenheit. Regardless of clothing, however prepared they might be, it would be impossible to remain in these temperatures for long without retreat to some sort of shelter.

For this and a second reason, he had determined that once the J7-V landed, he and Annie and Paul would strike immediately for The Retreat, in order to reach shelter and to ascertain whether or not Kurinami and Elaine Halversen had reached there.

If they had not, there was considerable likelihood they were dead by now. But he would find some means of making Annie stay behind in relative safety at the Retreat and set out with Paul using the truck, looking for them anyway.

The insulated snowpants already on, Rourke shouldered into his parka, almost instantly stifling in the warmth of the J7-V's fuselage.

Lieutenant Lintz's voice came over the speaker. "Doctor Rourke. We will be touching down in precisely five minutes. Please prepare to secure for landing."

Rourke checked his pockets, the insulated toque there, the snow goggles as well, the insulated gloves on top of the pack. "All right — Paul! Annie!"

"Right, daddy," Annie called back, sliding onto the bench-like seat, strapping in, Paul beside her. Rourke shoved his pack into a safe corner and sat flanking

Annie. "I hope we find them."

"And what's going on," Rourke added, securing the seat restraint.

CHAPTER ELEVEN

Michael Rourke reined back on the Asian horse under him, his eyes squinting against the full brightness of the sun, the stocky little gray bucking slightly, Michael knotting his fists into the coarse black of its mane, almost wrestling the animal into control.

"You look like your father without his sunglasses, your eyes half-closed against the sun like that," Otto Hammerschmidt said half through his teeth, reining in beside him, having more apparent difficulty with his mount than did Michael. The animal's hide ran from chestnut almost through black with every shade between somewhere represented, glistening with sweat at the flanks.

"We will be encountering their roving patrols soon," Han observed, handling his horse better than either Michael or Hammerschmidt. Michael wondered absently if it were just that Han Lu Chen knew better what to expect and, through anticipation, could counter the moves of the ill-tempered little creatures because of that. The other six men of the detail—three Chinese and three German, all enlisted personnel—formed a ragged semicircle around them.

"Better break out the banner, then," Michael Rourke suggested to Han.

"Agreed—although it will have very little effect, I

think," Han said, his voice even, emotionless, as though he were stating some obvious fact. Han swung out of the saddle easily, handing over his reins to Michael, Michael knotting his left fist more tightly into the gray's mane, Han's animal immediately beginning to squirm, tug at the reins Michael held now in his right.

The pack animal one of the three Chinese soldiers had led at the rear of the column stood docilely enough as Han dug beneath the covering over the pack saddle and produced a neatly rolled length of silk, the backs of embroidered lettering visible here and there. From the side of the pack saddle, Han took a pole some five feet in length, one end of the pole semi-sharp. He took a few paces back from the pack animal and stabbed the pole into the ground with considerable ferocity. But the ground was so hard that the pointed tip barely penetrated beyond, as it appeared from Michael's vantage point, anything more than two or three inches.

As if on cue, a gust of wind crossed the rock strewn gray plain on which they had paused, the deeper, almost purplish gray of the mountains jutting savagely upward in the distance, the mountains white-capped with snow from the approximate mid-point of their elevation. The gust of wind caught up the banner, unfurling it as Han began to affix the top of the banner to the staff. They were Chinese characters, embroidered in a deep blue against the field of pearl-cast white silk.

Michael Rourke could not read them, but knew their meaning nonetheless. The banner proclaimed that the riders came in peace, despite their weapons, in order to speak with the great leader of the Second City concerning a matter of grave importance. His indulgence was begged that they might be allowed to speak with him in an honorable fashion.

And Michael Rourke was beginning to wonder if his father's implication—that this was a fool's errand—

might not be true. In those mountains lurked the Mongol mercenaries who had been about to rape Maria Leuden, nearly caused Otto Hammerschmidt's death. Beside him, Otto's expression seemed to have deteriorated from serious to grim.

Han handed the banner to one of the Chinese soldiers, then took back the reins of his animal and moved into the saddle.

Michael reached beneath his leather jacket, taking out his gloves.

"We ride to the base of the mountains, Han?" Hammerschmidt asked.

"If we get that far, Captain Hammerschmidt," Han answered, digging in his heels and starting his mount ahead.

Michael grinned at Otto Hammerschmidt. "Well, he sure told you, didn't he?"

Hammerschmidt lit a cigarette in the cup he formed with his gloved hands, saying as he exhaled, "I was ordered to do this. Why are you here? Hmm? Who's the stupid one?" And Hammerschmidt laughed loudly as he signaled the six enlisted men, then spurred his mount after Han Lu Chen.

Michael held his animal back, watching after all of them for a moment. Han was by now a considerable distance ahead of the column composed of Hammerschmidt and his German/Chinese force, the banner suing for peace and diplomacy held high in the wind.

Michael's horse started to rear, Michael twisting the animal violently into obedience. His right hand drifted to the saddle scabbard and the M-16 there.

The man they went to see called himself Mao, after the iron-fisted totalitarian who ruled post World War Two Communist China. As Michael Rourke's hand lingered on the butt of the M-16, he recalled something Mao Tse Tung was credited with saying: "All power comes out of the barrel of a gun."

Michael Rourke dug in his heels, his animal coming instantly to a gallop, like a coiled spring released.

Mao's words made for sobering thoughts.

CHAPTER TWELVE

The J7-V hovered over the ice-packed, wind-hardened snow crust. The cloud of falling snow from the growing blizzard and tiny specks of loose ice swirled so densely around the machine and the three people who jumped from it that visibility extended barely beyond the length of John Rourke's reach.

His eyes were goggled, his face toqued, his head hooded, his hands gloved, but still the shock of cold penetrated almost to the bone as he reached out for Annie, Paul already having her by one arm, Rourke taking her by the other, both men leaning their bodies into the swirling snow and ice and wind and propelling her forward, the J7-V banking and slipping as it climbed, the ice and snow driving down on them now like microscopic daggers.

Rourke dragged his daughter ahead, Paul pushing her forward, Annie making some sort of barely intelligible sound, scream-like, but perhaps only the sound of labored breathing. Rourke's own breath came in cold gasps. He looked upward, his goggles almost instantly covered with a thin coating of snow and ice, the ice impacts against the plastic of the goggle lenses like a suddenly deafening cacophony which he felt through the bones in his face rather than heard; but the J7-V was banked nearly away. Rourke gathered his daughter in his arms, further attempts at movement pointless until the aircraft's cyclonic downdraft was abated.

Paul's hands protected her face and head. Rourke

embraced her closely. It had been a mistake to bring her here, but a mistake she had pushed for, beyond volunteering, insisted upon. They had been exposed for less than a minute. And bitterly, Rourke thought, if Kurinami and Halversen were out in this, they would be dead.

The downdraft from the German V-Stol aircraft was suddenly gone, Rourke shouting now over the keening of the wind, "We have to get moving! Annie? Will you be all right?"

"If everyone stops suffocating me by trying to protect me!"

He touched his covered-over lips to the hood of her parka and let her go, Paul shouting, "We have to get inside and out of this. The wind!"

Rourke nodded vigorously, not only for agreement's sake, but that his gesture be understood. He had shot a last minute azimuth on his compass before the aircraft had touched down, and he oriented himself now toward the ground and gestured and shouted, "Follow me!"

It was the wind, howling at gale force, which heightened the cold, made it penetrate despite the heaviest of outer garments. And his plotted course would soon take them into a defile. They would have to labor along its sides because of the depth of the snow—it was impossible to tell exactly how high because of the downdraft of the machine—but in the defile they would be out of the wind.

Paul began feeding out rope, Rourke using a carabiner clip to secure the leading end to his equipment, Annie six feet down its length and between them, then Paul clamping on, the remainder of the climbing rope coiled over his right shoulder.

Already, John Rourke was moving, his body leaning into the wind, he hoped shielding even marginally the effect of the wind on his daughter. He kept moving.

The drastic qualities of the weather here only deepened his concerns, developing over the last several weeks, that the climate was somehow eroding, as some had predicted it might. German high altitude observation craft had monitored band upon band of disturbances swiping toward the North American continent and toward Europe, Asia somehow shielded from the flow. But what was coming?

Rourke kept moving, the height of the snow more easily judged on the terrain over which they trudged, at least two feet or perhaps a bit more, but where the drifts were — which was all but everywhere — as high as four feet in places. Rourke's legs were already tired, but he felt no effects from the surgeries performed on him at Mid-Wake. The doctor, the techniques, all were peerless in his experience. He lifted his left leg, forced it down through the powder, then through the ice crust beneath and found footing, then the right leg, intentionally keeping his stride narrow so that Annie could follow in his footsteps and be spared the additional fatigue of carving out fresh ones. He glanced back once. She was a tall girl, but seemed pitifully small even by comparison to Paul, a slightly built man. She seemed all but lost inside the great folds of her parka and snowpants.

Rourke kept moving.

The defile was ahead. He quickened his pace, keeping his stride narrow though, not bothering to shout to Annie and her husband that the defile was near, barely having the breath for it if he had tried. Keeping moving was the thing. He did that. The defile was perhaps a hundred yards away now, Rourke bending his upper body so into the wind that as he placed one foot in front of the other, he sometimes began to lose his balance.

Almost without consciously realizing it, the height of the drifts began to decline, the force of the wind slacken. The torture of each step became slightly easier to endure. He reached the defile, trudging forward to get Annie and then Paul into its protection, then collapsing into the comparative warmth of the snow, the wind suddenly gone.

Annie sagged against him, and he couldn't tell if she cried or laughed . . .

Men in white snowsmocks—he assumed they were men—moved like spiders, their web a network of climbing ropes taking them along the face of the mountain which housed the Retreat, rather than along the road bed. One man would founder in the snow, be lost momentarily from sight, then appear, the others seeming almost to drag him onward for a time, then another man would endure the same. But through it all, they kept going.

Slung over the white snowsmocks were M-16 rifles and backpacks and carryalls and other gear.

John Rourke brought the binoculars down from his eyes and quickly drew his goggles back to protect his already numbing skin.

"What the hell are they doing?" Paul whispered loudly over the keening of the wind.

"Assaulting the Retreat, it appears," Rourke answered emotionlessly.

"Why? And who are they? From Eden?" Annie interjected, sounding incredulous.

"Evidently, Akiro and Elaine are inside the Retreat. Or at least our friends out there think they are. In either case, unless they're total imbeciles, they must be planning to plant explosive charges where they think the main entrance is. Aside from ourselves, only Kurinami and Halversen know the secret of the entrance. It seems safe to assume that if either of them had been captured, the secret of the entrance could have been extracted. If both of them had been captured, there would be no reason to penetrate the Retreat. Logic indicates they're both inside and that whoever sent these men knows it."

"Could conventional explosives do anything?"

Rourke shoved his hood back a little from his face, looking at Paul. "If the right kind of explosives were used and whoever planted them or instructed them to be planted had some engineering and geology skills to back him up, unfortunately so. Possibly more damage than they think. I built the Retreat to withstand everything except a direct hit, selected the site accordingly, but no location is completely insusceptible to explosive damage if the job is done correctly."

"Shit," Paul snarled.

"Indeed," Rourke nodded.

"Then what will we do?' Annie asked.

Rourke didn't answer her, but pulled down his goggles as the skies had caught fire. Almost as if they knew.

Rourke licked his lips beneath the covering of his toque.

He looked at his daughter and his best friend, her husband. "Somehow, I think they know about the escape tunnels, or at least the one which leads out onto the top of the mountain. I can't begin to fathom how they could, but it's the only logical conclusion. They're hauling explosives to the top of the mountain to blow their way in through the escape tunnel."

"Something we said—" Annie began.

"Anything we said wouldn't have betrayed the exact location. If they plant explosives all over the top of the mountain, that won't help them inside. They have to crack the double doors, otherwise they'd just be burying the tunnel entrance. Somehow, they know, it appears. So—"

"What do we do?" Paul asked.

"Even if Kurinami has the Retreat secured from inside — and I didn't show him how — he'll become aware of someone trying to enter. So, you can get inside without him letting you in or he'll let you in. Either way —"

"What are you doing?" Annie asked suddenly.

"I'm going up around the back side to the top of the mountain. I'll beat them by a good ten to fifteen minutes if I leave right away and they continue at their present rate of ascent. The two of you get to the main entrance and get inside, then secure the Retreat, Paul. I don't want anyone getting in through the front door just in case they know about that. Then Paul, you and Annie set up by the base of the tunnel leading to the top of the mountain. M-16s in a crossfire ought to do the trick in case they get past me."

"Suggestion?"

Rourke looked at Annie. "Suggestion."

"You and Paul take the back way around. I can get to the main entrance myself and I can get inside. I've done it before when I've had to. If Akiro and Elaine are inside, the three of us can keep guard at the base of the escape tunnel. With you and Paul going up top, there's less chance they'll ever make it through. And it doesn't take any great skills to put that escape tunnel entrance in a crossfire inside if we have to."

Rourke looked at his daughter and felt himself smile. "You're smart, you know that?" He looked at Paul. "You game? Why should I ask such a silly question." He hugged Annie for a brief instant. "Be careful. Go straight down there and if there's the slightest sign of any more of those guys, hide out until it's over. Understand?"

"If I were Michael you wouldn't say that."

"You're right — chiefly because he might not have sense enough to listen. Take off, sweetheart," and she embraced him, then Paul, then started along the defile, wading through drifts that were waist high to her, her

M-16 held high in both hands over her head.

Rourke looked at Paul as he — Rourke — recased his binoculars. "Ready?"

"Yeah," the younger man nodded.

Rourke was up, moving, along the width of the defile and starting up into the higher rocks. He glanced back once along the defile, but Annie was already through the narrow pass at the base and had disappeared . . .

"This is Weil. We rest for a moment. Secure your positions." He anchored his harness to the climbing rope, sagging back into a depression of rock where the snow was only partially drifted and he could, for a moment at least, escape the icy howling of the wind. His ears rang with it, what little there was of exposed flesh numb with it. Horst's vigil overlooking Rourke's mountain had yielded an interestingly promising result. Infrared emissions had indicated a marked difference in density at several locations along the mountain, beyond what Horst, a geologist by training, had considered normal. The story of Rourke on the last day before the ionization of the atmosphere had taken hold and the sky had caught fire was known to all by now, that he had used an escape tunnel and gone to the top of the mountain and from there, single-handedly, armed only with the little pistols he perennially carried, combated the last Soviet helicopter.

One of the anomalies Horst had detected was at the very crown of the mountain itself and, if they had any luck, the tunnel spoken of in the story.

Explosives such as they carried would crack through any artificial entranceway and then they would be able to penetrate the tunnel itself, utilizing more explosives at the base — because doubtless there was an interior door — and then the gas. The Japanese and his black mistress were too dangerous to be allowed to live.

There was always the threat that Rourke would, for some reason or another, return to his Retreat. Rourke or one of his armed and dangerous children or the Russian woman Rourke was so fond of. Weil discounted any true danger. Even if Rourke and three or four of his family were to return, they would be hopelessly outnumbered.

Weil looked to his weapon instinctively. The American M-16 was primitive, but satisfactory, although he would have preferred a weapon of German design, even one of similar vintage as these five centuries old museum pieces, perhaps the Heckler & Koch G-3. He had see these in the museums at New Germany, though never fired one. They appeared more substantial and, according to the data he had read on them, used a more substantial cartridge as well.

Weil mentally shrugged. The rockets he and his men carried would more than compensate for any shortcomings of their firearms, more than take care of this almost mythically endowed American, John Rourke. And then, work could progress to advance the cause of Nazism . . .

The snow made the going glower than Rourke had anticipated, so he quickened his pace against it, viewing the falling snow and the bitter cold of the winds almost as a human enemy, yet trying to account as best he could for the toll the exertion would take on him and not so hopelessly fatigue himself and Paul Rubenstein that, by the time they reached the top of the mountain, they would be too exhausted to fight. But it was imperative to attain the summit before the eight men with explosives reached it. "Hurry, Paul!"

"Right behind you."

It was necessary to raise his knees almost to the height of his waist in order to wade through the drifts, and the snow was very wet, uncharacteristic for Georgia at earlier time of his recollection, and so its very heaviness weighed against him. But John Rourke kept moving . . .

Annie Rourke fought through the drift since there was no way of getting over or around it, her arms too tired to keep the rifle anything more than chest height, the snow almost to her waist. It was necessary to plunge into it, then lift the legs as high as they would go, then plunge forward, compacting snow beneath the feet only to lift again and move perhaps two feet forward. Then repeat the process.

But ahead, she could see the entrance to the Retreat. It was coming home for her, the only real home she had known since she was a little girl. The difference in ages between herself and her brother were nothing now, but his memories of the incidents before the Great Conflagration were more detailed because he was two years older. And she didn't envy those memories, the time between the Night of The War and when the skies caught fire and all seemed ended and they took the Sleep as a last desperate gamble. It was hard for her to recall that interim period and the few years of normal childhood in anything more than generalities.

Annie Rourke Rubenstein could envision the Mulliner's dog and the farm field where, Michael told her, that they used to run and play. But how much of that vision was recollection, how much suggestion?

There were isolated, vivid memories of the house where they had lived before the Night of The War, memories of her mother's studio and the paintings that became the drawings used in the childrens' books Sarah

Rourke had written and illustrated, memories of warm smells in the kitchen, bread baking, cookies fresh from the oven.

But the other memories—the fear, the running, the hiding, the killing—she envied Michael not at all.

She stopped before the entrance to the Retreat and pushed back the hood of her parka, pulled down her goggles, undid the woolen scarf tied over her head, tore the toque away, her hair caught up in the wind, her face and throat and ears instantly as cold as ice, tingling. But if Akiro and Elaine were monitoring the entrance, they would recognize her that way. If not, she would attempt to open the door herself. If, somehow, Akiro had secured the entrance and she was not noticed, she would return to the rocks and wait in what shelter they would afford.

She would give it another two minutes before beginning to redon her headgear. If she could last that long. Already, her skin was numbing . . .

Prokopiev worked his way along the wall's base, the wall almost seeming to radiate tension. Senior Sergeant Piotr Yaroslav was just to Prokopiev's rear as he glanced back, the men following Yaroslav in a single file. Prokopiev's fists were balled tightly to his rifle at the pistol grip and small of the stock, this the newest version of the service rifle, issued just prior to the Hero Marshal's assault on the Underground City. Like its predecessor, it was modularly constructed, firing a caseless round as did all firearms of modern design. But it was constructed entirely of stainless steel, high strength aluminum alloys and polymers, the forty-round disposable magazines firing the 5.12mm X 35. The Vasonov-26 was state-of-the-art. He felt its art would be needed soon.

Beyond the wall lay a vast field, at its furthest extent,

perhaps a mile, the gray base of a mountain and visible in the mountain, the entryway to the Second Chinese City.

Prokopiev wanted battle, not reconnaissance. But duty was duty. He wanted to crush any and all Chinese for their betrayal of Communism, their support of what was then the United States during the critical period following the exchange of missiles and bombs. But the Comrade Colonel Antonovitch wanted their trust first, and then their destruction could come. Prokopiev would wait, would follow orders—at least for now. He kept moving . . .

The mountain top. John Rourke had climbed to it to raise the Stars and Stripes, shot it out with Rozhdestvenskiy, dove to the tunnel as the flames had closed around him. He had used the tunnel again, to see if there was a world at all remaining after he had first awakened from the Sleep.

He stood atop the mountain now, "lost in thought" the expression which came to mind, despite its triteness, accurate.

Paul Rubenstein stood beside him.

"I was never up here. You could see—in good weather you could—"

"A lot of Georgia. Into the Carolinas. When I built the Retreat, I never wanted it to be used for this. But I saw it coming Paul. God help me, I saw it coming."

"Mene, mene, Tekal upharson," Paul Rubenstein whispered.

"The handwriting on the wall," Rourke nodded, then started for the side along which the enemy climbers were coming.

CHAPTER THIRTEEN

John Rourke crouched beside the rocks near which he had stood bracing Rozhdestvenskiy five centuries before. But rather than a helicopter gunship, he waited for eight men. And this time, he was not alone, Paul Rubenstein hidden a few dozen yards off, prone behind ice-slicked boulders which had weathered millennia here. And fire did not well up to consume the skies now, snow and sleet driven on gale force winds swirling about the mountain top instead.

The Python in the full flap holster at his right hip was packed with snow between the rear of the trigger guard and the grip front strap, the flap not providing enough protection. He had left the Scoremasters in the back-pack, the pack hidden away closer to the far edge of the mountain top. But it would not come to guns immediately, perhaps, because if the attackers had kept to their climbing formation, only two of them at a time would reach the summit and to open fire would simply have alerted the others to trouble. It would be easy enough to shoot down at them on the rocks but there were a sufficient number of wide ledges along the face that the objects attached to their packs — rockets apparently — might be employed. And Rourke had no idea of their capabilities.

Had the Steyr-Mannlicher SSG been with him rather than left behind with Sarah at the First Chinese City, the proposition would have been little different. He would have been pushing the yardage to attempt, from hiding, to have picked the climbers off the mountainside rather than climb up to intercept them. And, the .308s the SSG fired would have behaved erratically in the high winds.

Instead, he waited, his right fist clenched tight to the haft of the Crain Life Support System X, the LS X his weapon of choice for the task at hand.

John Rourke saw the first of the climbers, the crown of a hooded head surfacing over the edge, then a hand groping, then both hands bracing and the chest visible, then all at once the white snowsmocked figure had attained the top. The man paused for the briefest instant, then turned back toward the face of the mountain, helping the second climber over the top.

Rourke's gloved right fist balled on the LS X.

He knew Paul would be watching for his move. He made it.

Rourke stood, stepped forward two paces, the first climber starting to turn around, Rourke's left hand going to the man's face, snapping the head and neck back and tensioning the head against the upper segment of the internal frame pack, Rourke's right hand driving forward. At the edge of his peripheral vision, he could see Paul Rubenstein, the Gerber Mk II in his right fist, hurtling himself toward the second climber, bulldogging the man to the ice-slicked surface as Rourke's own knife angled past the right side edge of the pack and punched through fabric and flesh and kidney and his left hand over the toque-covered mouth stifled the scream that the howl of the wind would have rendered otherwise inaudible.

The man sagged downward, knees buckling, Rourke guiding him to the ice as Rourke rammed the LS X further inward, upward. He could see Paul Rubenstein, straddling the second climber across the chest, the knife in Paul's right fist hammering down like a spike into the man's chest, wrenched free, then raking across the throat on the backswing, all movement from the man beneath Paul suddenly stopped in one violent spasm.

At once, Paul began dragging the body back into the rocks where it could not be seen, Rourke already doing the same. Rourke glanced toward the edge. Only seconds before more of them would be coming. But he had to know the capability of the rockets. Quickly, Rourke unlashed the one at the right side of the internal frame pack. He rubbed snow away from the rocket's casing, ice packed to it in a thin film, but some of the words visible on the tube. The words were in German. All thought of discerning more concerning the nature of the rocket itself vanished.

Rourke sagged forward for an instant, then looked over the dead man toward the edge of the mountaintop. Another climber. Rourke picked up the Crain knife, drew back deeper into the rocks, waited, his mind racing. Duplicity on the part of Colonel Wolfgang Mann and his leader, Deiter Bern? Rourke dismissed the thought. There was a firm bond of personal friendship between him and Doctor Munchen at the very least, even Hartman, the military commander with whom he had so closely worked. Rourke told himself he would have sensed something if he hadn't been told it.

If these men were Germans, why M-16s, Eden Project equipment doubtlessly? Why were they performing the evident bidding of Commander Christopher Dodd?

The climber was rising over the edge. And over the wind's howl as the man turned away toward the edge, Rourke could just make out the man's shout. "Weil— something is wrong here!" And the man's words were in German.

John Rourke was up, moving, driving his body forward toward the edge, his arm driving his knife forward still faster, Rourke's body slamming against the climber, pulling him down, Rourke's knifehand arcing around the man and driving the blade inward and downward through the chest at the man screamed.

Paul — Rourke saw the younger man moving toward the edge, the Gerber shifted into his left fist, the Schmeisser swinging forward, tensioning on its sling. Rourke let the dead man fall to the ice, the LS X still in him as Rourke's right hand let it go, arcing back to find the pistol grip of the M-16.

"Horst! Horst!" The call came from near the edge and Rourke dropped to his knees, the muzzle of the M-16 swinging up. "Horst!"

Paul Rubenstein dropped down beside him. "They're German, Paul," Rourke hissed, Paul Rubenstein's eyes widening beneath the snow goggles that he wore.

Rourke peered warily over the edge.

Again, the voice came, "Horst!" Then, a split second afterward, in German, the command to take cover.

Rourke shouted in German as well, leaning slightly over the edge so his words would carry. "Who are you?" But Rourke tucked back, no words answering him, only gunfire, a fusillade of assault rifle bullets ripping into the rock beside Rourke's face, Rourke averting his eyes, Paul Rubenstein snarling something at once incomprehensible yet abundantly clear in intent. The German MP-40 submachinegun was stabbed over the edge, firing a long burst downward toward the warren of ledges and overhangs below.

More assault rifle fire, Rourke stabbing the M-16 over the edge, firing it out in a long, ragged, zigzagging burst, then pulling back, Paul beside him. "What the hell do we do now?"

Before Rourke could answer, there was a barely audible hiss, but the sound, despite its lack of volume, sufficiently different from the constant wailing of the wind and the tinkling sounds of blowing ice pellets that he heard it. Rourke threw himself toward Paul and dragged them both down, the mountaintop around them vibrating under the impact as — it had to be one of the rockets — the explosion came, so loud Rourke's ears rang with it, his body so shaken that his skeleton almost resonated with it.

Rourke pushed himself up, clumps of snow tumbling from the hood of his parka, his rifle half-buried in it.

Rourke's right hand found the Python, no time to reach the Detonics Combat Masters under his cold weather gear, ripping the Metalifed and Mag-na-Ported Colt .357 from the leather, more snow impacted around the area of the trigger guard. Rourke pulled down his toque and blew it out, swinging the muzzle on line toward the edge of the drop as the first of the climbers became visible. Rourke double actioned the revolver once, into the chest of the first man.

Paul Rubenstein was moving now, the Schmeisser gone as he sat up, Rourke seeing him at the far left edge of his peripheral vision. Paul's hands filled with the M-16 that had been slung on his back, an uneven burst cutting across the snow in front of the second man to rise to the mountaintop, the man's M-16 already firing. But as the second man stepped back, his balance went and he started to career backward, Rourke firing into the man's throat, the body sailing back over the edge.

Three of the climbers remained. No more were coming, but heavy assault rifle fire was coming from over the side, peppering the lip of the summit, ricochets bouncing off the rocks around them as Rourke staggered to his feet, the Python clenched in his right fist, his left hand groping in the snow for the M-16 . . .

Annie Rourke Rubenstein had started into the snow

when the vibration of the explosion had rung through the Retreat walls like a clapped bell, throwing her arctic parka on over her sweater, an M-16 in each hand, Kurinami behind her. She had run to the monitor console, the lens of the camera at the summit partially obscured with snow and ice; but she was barely able to see her father and her husband, collapsed as a shower of snow and rock debris rained down around them, the fireball of some tremendous explosion still dissipating skyward. She shouted to Elaine Halversen now as she ran through the interior doorway, "Close the doors — keep the Retreat closed unless you see us on camera and we're all right!"

Kurinami had no coat, but his right hand held an M-16, his left a Beretta 92F, a knife almost as impossibly long as her father's LS X sheathed beside his left hip.

Annie didn't know exactly what she would do as she exited through the doorway, the cold biting into her like steel, her hands almost instantly numbing on the pistol grips of her rifles. They had been waiting beside the entrance to the escape tunnel which led to the top of the mountain when the explosion had come, and suddenly she had realized that waiting was no longer possible. Her glimpse of the video monitor had confirmed that.

She was running now, her hair blown across her face and over her eyes like a heavy veil, running toward what before the Awakening had been the garden in which she had grown the tobacco for her father's cigars. "Rolled on the hip of a virgin," he had teased her afterward. She was not any more, and there had been no more time to make cigars. But from the vantage point of the garden spot, she would be able to lay down a heavy volume of fire onto the mountain's face where the climbers had been. If they were the origin of the explosion — logic dictated they were — perhaps she could prevent a second one. She slipped and fell, her mouth filling with snow, her hair wet with it, her hands now so totally numb that she wondered on one level of consciousness if she would still be able to pull the triggers of her weapons. She pushed herself up, stumbling, fighting her way forward through the drifts, Kurinami just ahead of her. "The garden! Fire up at them from the garden, Akiro!"

Did he know where the garden was? Yes—he would have seen it when he and Elaine had first visited the Retreat when they were the first man and woman to return to earth from the Eden Project shuttles. Inside herself, she had always thought it was so romantic that Akiro and Elaine had fallen in love, that they planned to marry, like Adam and Eve in a way, the first man and first woman.

She kept running, falling again, pulling up the hood of her parka as she rose, the hood filled with snow and spilling down the back of her neck where her hair had blown over, down inside her sweater and under her blouse, chilling her still more. Annie picked herself up, kept running.

She could hear assault rifle fire, as if far away and above. Was it her father and her husband, answering the fire of the climbers, or the climbers themselves?

And then she heard the crack of a neat three round burst from an M-16, the crack of it on the cold air over the keening of the wind earsplittingly loud.

Akiro Kurinami, firing toward the mountainside and the climbers there.

Annie half-stumbled to her knees near him, shouldering one of the M-16's, dropping the other into the snow, trying to move her right thumb enough to work the selector, getting it to the auto position, then moving her right first finger against the metal of the trigger, flesh blistering to metal. She opened fire toward the rock face, Kurinami's rifle blazing beside her. The distance was too great for any real accuracy. And the angle was bad. She kept firing anyway, hoping for a lucky shot . . .

John Rourke had the M-16 in his gloved left fist, Paul Rubenstein beside him, the volume of gunfire increased from the rock face, some of it strangely hollow, almost distant.

"Annie?" Paul hissed through chattering teeth.

"Come on!" Rourke was up, slipping once, catching his balance, moving toward the edge now, Paul Rubenstein beside him. If Annie was firing at them from the ground, it would be a matter of seconds before the climbers would utilize one of their rockets against her. And this time, the rocket couldn't help but claim its target.

Rourke fell prone by the edge of the rock face, ramming the M-16 over the side, firing it out, Paul beside him, doing the same.

Rourke peered over the edge for an instant, then gunfire tearing into the rocks beside him. But he saw three climbers remaining, the leadman suspended from a rope cramponed into the rock face perhaps a hundred feet down. Another of the men was — awkwardly — readying one of the rocket tubes for firing.

Rourke rolled onto his back, pulling his toque back up over his mouth, his chin numbing with the cold.

The second man he had killed with his knife — the body, partially covered with blown up snow and rock debris — lay only a few feet from him, eyes wide open in death and slowly covering with fallen snow, the haft of Rourke's knife and the double quillion guard and the blade stem almost cross-shaped over him.

Rourke handed off his M-16 to Paul Rubenstein, stabbing the Python into the flap holster and closing it. Then he skidded on his knees toward the dead man, wrenching the knife free. "Paul! I'm going down — to cut their rope. Get both of those loaded and cover me. It's the only chance." Rourke sheathed the knife.

He didn't wait for an answer, the scraping of magazines out of and into magazine wells the only answer needed, the thwacking sounds of the magazines being seated.

Rourke was at the edge. There was a diagonally sloping shelf, ridged as if some vastly harder rock had gouged across it, the ridges ice filled and slicked, this immediately below him, one solitary piton — no crampon could have been placed there — set near the center. "Now!" Rourke shouted, rolling over, the rock surface tractionless, his footing gone for one terrifying instant, his body skidding laterally, his arms and legs spread-eagling, finding a purchase. He started creeping downward, skidding again, his right arm lashing out, his right first closing around the piton, his body swinging from it pendulum-like.

Rourke flipped over onto his back, his mind racing, the gunfire still coming from the foot of the mountain. And in a moment, he knew, there would be the whooshing sound of a rocket being fired, and if it were Annie down there — it had to be — she would be dead. Gunfire from above, Paul Rubenstein firing through the defile, toward the climbers below.

Rourke's left hand edged to his pistol belt, opening the buckle, ice and snow clotting it, his hand holding it at the buckle end. As he tugged at the belt, what he knew would happen happened, what was unavoidable because there was no time to prevent it happening, because his left hand couldn't even reach to the gun and snatch it from the leather and secure it in his waistband, his body so distended, the flap holster with the Python inside it sliding free of his belt, holster and gun skidding down along the rock face, disappearing over the edge —

106

gone forever? But his daughter's life was at stake. Rourke had the belt, nothing else on it this time out, his left fist tight over the buckle as he swung his arm outward and upward, almost contacting his right hand.

Rourke swung his left arm again, hand contacting hand, the buckle going over the piton, his left first balling in the leather, then his right as he let go of the piton. Quickly, because time was gone, Rourke edged downward.

He was at the base of the long, sloping ledge and he found a purchase for his feet, letting go, wedged there, the rope that was the climbers' lifeline perhaps fifty feet below him now. He started down, hand over hand, his left hand slipping, his body skidding along the rock surface, his right booted foot ramming into a ledge, shale and ice dislodging, his descent slowing, his left hand finding a groove in the rock surface. He was stopped. Rourke looked down. Another twenty feet, gunfire coming toward him, chipping the rock face near his hands and feet and near his face. More gunfire from above. Paul. And gunfire from the base of the peak— Annie! Rourke kept moving downward, the rope vibrating under the weight of the climbers who clung to it, the missile tube fully extended, to the shoulder of the bottom man perhaps fifty yards below.

There was no time left. Rourke turned his back to the mountain, almost tearing open his parka, biting off his right outer glove through the toque over his mouth, his inner-gloved right hand finding the butt of the Detonics mini gun under his left armpit, ripping it from the Alessi leather, his thumb jacking back the hammer.

Rourke stabbed the pistol downward toward the man with the rocket tube, firing, then again and again, the man's body seeming to go rigid, then the tube falling from his right shoulder, going into the abyss below where the Python had vanished, the body flopping outward and away from the rock face, the climbing rope shuddering. Rourke looked to the rope, answering gunfire coming from below him, his eyes behind the goggles squinting involuntarily against the rock spray, his face turning away, his shoulders hunching.

More gunfire from above, and he thought he heard Paul's voice shouting a warning. Rourke stabbed the Detonics .45 outward and fired, toward the two crampons from which the climbing rope was suspended. His first shot rocked one of the crampons free of the rock, the rope snapping downward, his second shot a miss, only one shot remaining. There was no chance to grab at the second Combat Master. Rourke settled the muzzle, front and rear sights on line. As a hail of assault rifle fire from the two still living climbers impacted the rock face around him, his right first finger twitched against the trigger, the little stainless pistol rocking in his hand, the 185-grain jacketed hollow point whining as gilding metal coated lead impacted high tensile strength steel and the rock into which it was set, the crampon rocketing away from the mountainside, the rope snaking outward, a scream from below him piercing the night air, a last burst of assault rifle fire, two men falling away below him.

John Rourke closed his eyes, his head sagging back against the cold of the rock face.

CHAPTER FOURTEEN

They had pressed on from their uneasy campsite in the shadow of the mountains which sheltered the Second City, even the tiny Pryzwalski-like horses they rode seeming to sense the imminent danger, more unsettled than during the previous day's ride.

Michael Rourke rode beside Han Lu Chen, whose family had died at the hands of Second City invaders, stonily silent, Otto Hammerschmidt riding drag with two of the six enlisted men of their force, one of the men Chinese, the other German.

The mountains which had been distant and gray now seemed twice their original size, the gray deeper but with more pronounced shadings and the granite upthrustings almost menacingly close.

There was light snow here and the wind was driving harder, through the niches between the rock chimneys making eerie whistling sounds, and when a stronger gust blew and the unearthly howling seemed unnaturally heightened, the animals would shudder and hesitate, edging nervously right or left. At these times, it was more necessary than usual to hammer at the animals' sides with the knees, to dig in the heels and urge them unwillingly ahead.

Michael Rourke was reminded of the Valley of Death from the Twenty-third Psalm, but it was not a valley into which they had ridden, kept riding now.

At last, Han spoke. "They will know we are here.

They will be waiting for us. But perhaps we can kill some of them."

"If you have such a lack of faith in this, why are you here? Orders only?"

"If Mao and his cutthroats and that evil bitch, his mistress, do not ally with us, they will ally with the Russians and then there will be nuclear war. It is better to die for one insane chance than to die huddled in a hole, I think."

"I've seen nuclear war. You're right," Michael answered, almost whispering.

Michael's mount shuddered violently, all but refusing to proceed, Han reining in a few feet ahead, the animal Han rode rearing slightly, Han fighting it down.

Michael Rourke licked his lips, looking upward into the rocks. There had been no howl of wind, no death-like whistling. His eyes squinted and for a fleeting instant, he thought he detected movement in the rocks above to his left.

"Han—up there? Did you see it?"

"I saw nothing, Michael, but that means nothing."

Michael Rourke dug in his heels and the animal beneath him vaulted ahead, reared, swinging left, Michael leaning hard forward over the saddle, hands knotting in the animal's mane . . .

Prokopiev looked at Yaroslav and then spoke into his helmet mounted radio headset. "This is Prokopiev. The riders are entering the killzone. On my command, all elements open fire. Be ready."

Prokopiev settled the small of his rifle's stock more comfortably into his left hand, waiting, watching as the two men in civilian clothes and the seven others, almost evenly divided between two uniforms (four of the uniforms recognizable as German), rode ahead.

"Be ready, Comrades," Prokopiev hissed.

The riders were coming. With the Chinese army advancing he and Yaroslav and the men of his force had all but encountered them several miles distant. The horses of the men in the gorge below them were the only obstacle against rendezvousing with the extraction helicopters. Even if the gunfire were heard, as well it might be, the Chinese army was on horseback as well.

Prokopiev had never ridden a horse, doubted that any of his men ever had, but the horses could be ridden, even a few of them, the rest of his force staying behind to hold off the enemy forces while others went to meet the gunships that were to extract them, then come back with the gunships. There was no possibility of radio contact with the gunships, because they would be out of range and under enforced radio silence. But, Prokopiev smiled, either he or old Yaroslav could "persuade" the pilots to fly back for the others and engage the Chinese forces if necessary, even if they couldn't be lawfully ordered to do so. That, or shoot the pilots and take the helicopters and fly them themselves. He could explain it away to Comrade Colonel Antonovitch.

"Remember, Comrades," Prokopiev hissed into his headset. "Do not kill the horses. Open fire on my command." Prokopiev blinked his eyes several times, began to regulate his breathing as he cheeked tighter to the rifle's straightline buttstock . . .

Michael Rourke felt it inside him, an uncomfortable feeling as if some other sense beyond the normal five were operation. Was he becoming like Annie?

But he felt something.

"Wait, Han."

Han reined back. Michael Rourke looked up into the rocks flanking them. "Ever hear of 'The Lone Ranger'?"

"Who?"

"Nothing—but somehow—"

The first shots rang out, a burst of sharp cracking assault rifle fire echoing and re-echoing among the rocks so rapidly, so loudly that it was impossible to tell its origin, one of the Chinese soldiers going down from the saddle, his horse rearing, falling. And as Michael Rourke reached for his M-16, he shouted, "Remind me to tell you the story sometime!" Otto Hammerschmidt, who had been riding with his rifle in his hand, was returning fire, as were the three other Germans who had ridden the same way.

Michael's own horse began to rear, Michael fisting the rifle as he threw his right leg over the saddle horn and knotted his fists in the reins and mane, the all-but worthless animal's neck twisting at an unnatural angle as it tumbled gracelessly to the unyielding ground. Michael Rourke threw himself behind it, firing his M-16 wildly up into the rocks, gunfire general now, Han's horse wheeling, Han firing a pistol toward the rocks on either side of the gap.

One of the German soldiers went down, his horse spilling head over heels, the German's body unwillingly cartwheeling away, the rifle skidding across the rocks and gravel.

The story, if he lived to tell Han about it, dealt with a massacre in a gap like this, but in Texas, thousands of miles and six centuries ago, long before men had ever thought about nuclear warfare and its barbaric, tenuous aftermath. Michael Rourke kept shooting.

CHAPTER FIFTEEN

He had found his Python, the Metalife finish unscathed, but the cylinder impacted out of the frame, the rear sight broken off and the barrel sprung, or wrenched out of true with the frame, as he had described it. Gun and holster had become separated during the tumble from the mountaintop.

Annie poured her father a drink, he and Paul fresh from another forty-five minutes in the arctic-like temperatures searching the bodies of the climbers and searching for the lost, now recovered but irreparably damaged, revolver.

Was this whiskey more of the Seagram's Seven or was it some of the whiskey he had gotten the Germans to duplicate for him and which—according to Michael—he had put into the original, centuries old bottles? They had duplicated his pet Federal loads for the family's firearms, had duplicated parts and lubricants and all sorts of items.

She sipped at the glass she had poured for herself. It tasted the same as Seagram's Seven had always tasted, but it would have, of course, or her father would not have wasted his time bringing it to the Retreat. It was a gross understatement, but John Thomas Rourke was a man of definite tastes.

Annie Rubenstein took two glasses in hand and walked back toward the sofa which dominated the center of the great room, setting two down, then going back to the kitchen counter, up the three steps, Elaine having poured the other two glasses. Annie took her own glass, sipping at it again, not rejoining them, watching them as Elaine brought her own and Akiro's drink to the low table and set them down, then settled onto the floor at Akiro's feet.

Annie set down her drink, burrowing her hands into the slit pockets at the sides of the ankle length black full skirt she had changed into, a shawl cocooned around her shoulders over the open collared gray blouse, her black stockinged feet in flat-soled Icelandic walking shoes.

She felt almost human again, and physically more comfortable. She had showered under steaming hot water (thank God Akiro had activated the water-heating system) and changed when it had proven useless that she might argue her way into accompanying her father and her husband back into the storm, as Akiro had.

Elaine had stood by the bathroom door, talking idly while Annie had scrubbed hair and body under the steaming spray, just letting her innermost being thaw out, unwind. "Why are they trying to kill you and Akiro, Elaine? I mean, what's behind it, Commander Dodd?"

"I think it's because of the computer files. They were wiped out, but Akiro had made copies before that, just in case—duplicates, you know?"

"Uh-huh—and they want the duplicates?—I mean, Dodd wants them?"

"I think that was it at first, but I think they gave up on that and decided their ends would be served just as well if Akiro and I were dead and nobody at all knew where the duplicate files were hidden."

"Where are they hidden, Elaine?"

114

"Akiro buried the copies he made about halfway between Eden Base and the German installation. You don't think it was the Germans, do you? I mean, they've helped all of us so much and all—"

"No—I don't think it was the Germans. Did I remember to put out a towel?" She knew that she had, but she had wanted to change the subject and the momentary casual question had accomplished that.

Annie fished her left hand from her pocket now and took up her drink. It was strange, but she'd put ice cubes into it. She had been so cold and she was having a drink and she used ice cubes. She wondered if humans were just simply insane?

And an annoying feeling had been invading her thoughts; there had been no chance to mention it to Paul, and she didn't want to add the doubt it would sow to her father's already overwhelming burden: Natalia, her own mother and the baby, the problems of Akiro and Elaine with Commander Dodd—all of that. And now her father's revolver destroyed. But she sensed, no matter how she tried to fight it, that Michael was somehow in danger.

Annie took a healthy swallow of her drink and the feeling still didn't ebb away. She walked down toward the sofa, listening as her father talked.

"So you think Dodd is up to something with some unknown group of conspirators? Correct?"

"Yes, Doctor Rourke." Akiro Kurinami answered almost deferentially.

Paul was trying to struggle out of his boots and Annie set down her drink and settled to her knees at his feet. "Let me do that," she whispered, her voice low so she would not interrupt her father, her hands becoming busy with the boot laces, her mind busy with her father's words, but the nagging thoughts of Michael being in some sort of danger penetrating her thoughts like rapier thrusts. She almost had the first boot off, Paul leaning back, evidently enjoying her domesticity, which was why she had volunteered to remove his boots from him in the first place. Men wanted little things like that done for them, and liked it even when they didn't deserve it. Paul deserved it.

Annie began untying the second boot.

Her father again began to speak. "Those men were probably German. No identification, of course, but one of them was named Weil and another of them called out for a man named Horst, evidently the third fellow we killed on the mountaintop. The rifles were M-16s—I'd venture to say the serial numbers would match up to some of those missing from the Eden supplies. The handguns were German, the rocket launchers German, but the launchers not something I've seen in current German military inventory. Possibly something superceded and put out as surplus, more likely stored and subsequently stolen. I'd say, just as a guess, that they're Nazis."

"Nazis?" Elaine Halversen seemed to gasp the word.

"Nazis again," Paul said dispiritedly, Annie looking up from her knees at him as he spoke. He had pretty eyes. She pulled off his second boot, then curled up at his feet, putting his feet up into her lap to warm them and her hands, curling her legs under the fullness of her skirt. He smiled down at her as she raised her eyes toward him, Annie feeling his hand touch gently at the hair at the nape of her neck.

It was good to be married, even better to be in love.

"When Colonel Mann crushed the Nazi Party in New Germany, it was only to be expected that the closet Nazis, or some of the ones who swore allegiance to Deiter Bern weren't 'reconstructed', as they used to say," her father began again. "It would have been impractical at the least to attempt any sort of spiritual alliance with the Communists, but someone at the German installation outside Eden Base could have sounded out Dodd, then laid out a deal. I never trusted Commander Dodd very far. If power was waved in front of him, as evidently it was, as well as the promise of unlimited access to German technology, it's well within the realm of probability that he succumbed."

Annie spoke. "But what could he have offered them in return, daddy?"

Her father looked down at her and smiled. "I'm just guessing, sweetheart, but I think the best thing he had to offer was a little legitimacy. He'd give the Nazis something they could work through, like in the old days when organized crime would buy into legitimate businesses or unions just so there was a front operation they could hide behind." And the corners of her father's mouth drew out and downturned, but his eyes smiled. "We may be sitting in at the dawn of a new era in perfidy."

Annie felt Paul's fingers tense against her neck for the briefest instant. She took her drink from the table and swallowed half of it, then leaned her head against Paul's right knee and closed her eyes for a moment.

CHAPTER SIXTEEN

Michael Rourke had six full thirty-round magazines and two partially empty ones. The contents of these latter, as he quietly assessed the situation, his M-16 across his squatted legs, he combined into one magazine. At the distance, handguns were useless noise-makers and a knife was mere wishful thinking.

Fighting their way into the rocks on the far west end of the gap had been bought only through the wounding of another of the Chinese soldiers. But barricaded here as they were, it was impossible for the attackers on the west end of the gap to shoot down on them because of the overhang and the only enemy fire that could reach them was from the rocks on the eastern side of the gap. The range between the so far anonymous ambushers and the position from behind with Michael Rourke, Han Lu Chen, Otto Hammerschmidt and the others, including one of the wounded, returned fire was at least two hundred yards. There seemed to be no immediate danger of being attacked from the rear by the enemy force above.

Michael Rourke was reminded of the term "stand-off" and shared that insight with the Chinese intelligence agent and the German commando captain. "A 'stand-off', as the term was used, was a situation in which neither party could gain the advantage, nor conveniently disengage."

"That summarizes it well. Who are they, do you

think?" Hammerschmidt rasped through a cloud of cigarette smoke. "This Mao character's Mongol mercenaries or the Russians?"

"Russians, I think," Han said softly. "The Mongols wouldn't have been denied the blood sport of riding down on us, even for a tactical advantage. And the Mongols would have shot the horses. Whoever is up in those rocks—Russians is my estimate—wants the horses alive. Notice how carefully they avoided firing at you for example, Michael, when you brought your horse down and fired from behind it." The animals they had ridden, and the pack animal, grazed some distance away, where the snow covering was thin and there was some sparse ground cover, brown and dead, but evidently sufficiently tempting to keep them from bolting further away beyond the gap despite the sporadically noisy interchanges of gunfire. "We cannot go forward, nor can we go back," Han concluded with an air of finality.

Michael Rourke had rescued his rifle, his saddle bags, his water bottle and his sleeping bag, which was now warming one of the injured enlisted men. Inside the saddle bags was a medical kit, most of the contents already used in the preliminary treatment of the injured. Like his father, he had taken to carrying a musette bag almost constantly, inside it additional medical supplies which his father had carefully taught both he and his sister, Annie, how to use to stay alive. But advanced first aid training was not adequate to saving the lives of the wounded and the condition of the German who had been shot off his horse in the first instants of battle was deteriorating rapidly.

Michael Rourke, as a volley of automatic weapons fire from the eastern side of the gap subsided, shouted over the rock barricade, "Who are you?"

There was total silence, except for the eerie whistling of the wind among the jagged gray rocks surrounding them. But then a voice broke the silence, the English heavily accented, the accent unmistakably Russian, but the English none-the-less quite syntactically correct. "I am Major Vassily Mikhailovitch Prokopiev. I take it that you sue for surrender terms. To whom do I speak?"

"Bastard," Hammerschmidt snarled under his breath.

Despite the situation, Michael Rourke laughed. Then he shouted back to the Russian, "I am Michael Rourke." He had debated whether or not, if these were Russians, to reveal his true identity; but to conceal it seemed pointless. The present situation was one step away from the grave. "We do not sue for terms that we might surrender to you, but instead offer you and your men a guarantee of fair treatment on condition of your surrender."

Michael tucked back down, waited.

Laughter reverberated from the rocks on the eastern elevation of the gap, but that was to be expected. Without changing position, Michael shouted back, "Go ahead and laugh, Major Prokopiev. When my father, Doctor John Rourke, and the rest of the German-Chinese force arrives, let's hope you'll find that amusing as well."

Michael Rourke said nothing more, but neither was there any more gunfire. He felt it might be wise to explain the American term "bluff" to his compatriots. But he'd save that for later. "If the Russians weren't interested in shooting our horses," he began, looking at Hann and Otto Hammerschmidt, "then the logical inference, if we can assume they aren't all dedicated animal rights activists, is that they require the horses, which may, in fact, be the purpose of the attack. Clearly, they're in what would have to be considered enemy territory with Mao's armies on the loose. What if our friends up in the rocks need our mounts in order to escape a pursuing force from the Second City? Hmm?"

"That would make sense," Hammerschmidt said, almost as if to himself. "What if we shot the horses?"

"If there is a Second City army pursuing these Russians," Han said hastily, "I would be loathe to encounter them on foot. Assuming we do make it out of this, some of us at least, horseback is our only chance. And if these Russians have somehow provoked Mao's wrath, we may not even have the opportunity to show the peace banner and be laughed at and disregarded. We will be slaughtered before they come sufficiently close to read it."

Michael followed Han's eyes to the rocky surface at the approximate center of the gap. The meticulously embroidered banner lay there, flapping in the wind, useless. "If they want our horses, they're trying to get to a rendezvous. Helicopter gunships, probably. This could be a reconnaissance patrol for a larger force. Shit," Michael rasped.

The stalemate was still unchanged, despite having possibly deduced a rationale for it.

He gambled again, raising his voice to shout across the gap to the Soviet commander. "Prokopiev! How close is the army from the Second City? Think they've heard the gunfire yet? Think they're going to come more quickly now? Think you have a chance alone against them? We'll shoot our horses first!"

There was a long silence, punctuated only by the wind, Hammerschmidt lighting another cigarette, Han's eyes darting nervously to the opposite side of the gap.

And then Prokopiev's voice came. "Will you meet with me down there beside your banner?"

Michael looked to the floor of the gap where the banner lay, then up into the rocks on the eastern side.

"Once you step out into the open, what is to stop them from cutting you down?" Hammerschmidt whispered hoarsely, snapping his cigarette butt from his fingers.

"If we do not do something," Han said softly, "we shall all be dead. But I will go instead," Han declared.

Michael Rourke looked at both men, then back toward Prokopiev's position. "Five minutes. You come armed and so will I, and that way if anyone tries any treachery, the other will assuredly die."

"Agreed, Rourke. Five minutes."

Michael consulted the time as he leaned his M-16 against the rocks behind which he crouched, then began removing the spare magazines for it from his gear. He ripped one of the Beretta 92F military pistols from his shoulder holster, perfunctorily checking its condition of readiness even though he already knew it, re-holstering it, performing the same operation with its twin. "I'll leave my rifle. There wouldn't be time to use it out there. If Prokopiev brings a rifle, so much the better. Slower to get into action." He withdrew the four-inch Model 629 from the holster at his side, opened the cylinder. "I don't know what's going to go down out there, so be ready to follow my lead." He closed the .44 Magnum revolver's cylinder, re-holstering it as well.

"I should go—" Han insisted.

"No. You know your way out of here. You can speak Chinese in case we do get to Mao's forces or they get to us. If I can convince him my father is coming, after what my dad and Natalia did to Karamatsov, it might buy us out of here. And Prokopiev wouldn't have reacted so quickly if he didn't have some sort of force from the Second City breathing down his collar. No—this is the only way."

Michael looked at his Rolex. It was nearly time. "If he tries anything, he dies," Hammerschmidt announced, his voice emotionless.

"If he tries anything, we might all die," Michael interjected, standing up slowly, keeping his hands in plain view, but the leather jacket open so he could get at the Berettas.

"Good luck!" Han hissed.

Michael Rourke anticipated needing it as he stepped from behind the rocks and into the open. Prokopiev—Michael assumed it was the Soviet commander—was coming down from the rocks, a never before seen assault rifle slung crossbody beneath his right arm, a pistol holster at his belt, the uniform the black battle dress utilities of the KGB Elite Corps, jump boots rather than jackboots. Prokopiev was tall, about Michael Rourke's own height, lean and well muscled. He began walking out.

Michael Rourke walked slowly toward the center of the gap, matching his pace to Prokopiev's so they would arrive beside the fallen banner at approximately the same moment.

"You have no rifle," Prokopiev shouted, his voice edged with humor.

Michael kept walking, calling across to him as he

did, "I don't need one, Major."

Prokopiev stopped beside the banner. Michael stopped less than a yard from him. "So," Michael grinned, "who's running the Elite Corps these days?

Prokopiev smiled. "I am."

Michael was momentarily taken aback, but countered in the next instant. "Personnel shortage with everyone promoting themselves since Karamatosov died, is there?"

"You intend to provoke me, Rourke?"

"No — not really. It was a cheap shot. Antonovitch take over?"

"Yes. The comrade colonel shall avenge the murder of the Hero Marshal."

"And you intend to help him," Michael said, making a statement, not a question.

"Indeed, Rourke."

Michael nodded thoughtfully. "If the Chinese catch up with you before you touch base with your own people, well — that may be just a hope and nothing more." He was consciously attempting to keep his English as idiomatic as possible, thereby hopefully confusing this man enough that if he — Michael — overstepped his guesswork, it might go undetected.

"What is it that you propose, Rourke?"

"Michael is fine. My friends call me that. I imagine some of my enemies do, too. I'll shoot you the straight shit, Vassily — may I call you that?"

"If you like." There was a hard edge to Prokopiev's voice, but it was tinged with uncertainty.

"Good. We were on our way to the Second Chinese City in order to open negotiations with this Mao character. We want an alliance with him if we can get it. That should be obvious at any event. You want his

124

access to the pre-War Chinese nuclear arsenal and we don't want you to have it. Let's be honest about it. But with this gunfire, with some of our people wounded, with you guys around, I don't think now is the right time to go visiting. Especially since you probably have an attack force of your own en route to this area and you were on an intelligence gathering mission. Right?"

"Go on," Prokopiev hissed.

"I've got a substantial force of German and Chinese troops—from the First City—right behind us. That might not do us any good, though, if Mao's people are too close to you. You've got a rendezvous to keep, but you won't reach it in time to save your bacon without our horses. If you get our horses, we're stuck here as the reception committee for Mao's army. I was explaining to my heavily armed friends back there in the rocks," and Michael jerked a thumb toward the position he had just left, "that this is a 'stand-off': A tactical situation that has stalemated. The way it is now, nobody wins or loses and we all wait here like sitting ducks for Mao's people to come along and kill us, or worse."

"What is it that you propose—Michael? I take it that you have prepared some solution to this situation, although I do not agree that it is this—stand-out thing."

" 'Stand-off', Vassily. But you're just hanging tough. I admire that. You have us trapped, but your people can't get to the horses while we can pick you off. If we keep shooting at one another long enough, Mao's people are going to come that much faster and there's a substantial chance the horses will run out of grazing and wander off. And, if your people haven't ridden before, they'll never control those horses. Nasty little critters, believe me. I've been a horseman since before the Night of The War, and I have a hard time controlling them."

"What is it that you propose?"

Michael looked toward the horses, pausing for what he hoped was dramatic impact. "You have people waiting for you. We have people waiting for us. You probably have more men than we have horses, right?"

Prokopiev paused for an instant, then his eyes—they were gray—flickered. "We do."

"So you planned to kill us, take our horses and leave some men behind for a holding action, then get back and bail them out, right?"

"You mean rescue them? Yes. This was the plan. It will still work."

Michael shook his head, smiled, "Vassily—Vassily—look—My plan is this. We have a temporary truce; I suggest expanding it and working together until the crisis is resolved. I'll pledge my word that if our people arrive first, you'll go unmolested. And I'll accept your word of the same."

"You are insane!"

"No—and you know I'm not. We have seven horses. Eight with the pack animal. I propose that two of our guys and two of your guys head for help to their respective forces. We hold the other four horses in reserve just in case. We take positions on the high ground on both sides of the gap here. That way, we can still start shooting at one another if we want. But we'll also have the gap bottlenecked and can hold back Mao's people—or try to at least—until help arrives, your people or ours. And if you have a medical technician who's got field surgery experience, we have one of our wounded who's dying. Our boys will teach your boys how to handle those horses. With men going in two different directions to two possible sources of help, we're doubling the chances that we'll make it out of this alive. What do you say?"

Vassily Prokopiev began to laugh; at this stage, Michael Rourke didn't know if that were a good thing or a bad thing. He didn't say anything. And abruptly, the KGB Elite Corps Commander stopped laughing. "You are serious."

"Deadly serious. What about it?"

Prokopiev looked to the still grazing horses, Michael following his eyes. As if on cue, the animals began edging further away. "You have my word. A sizeable force is perhaps two hours behind us now. We should get on with this at once."

"I'll get two riders. You get two. Send over your surgeon and call your men out of the rocks over us. You and I can help wrangle the horses."

"Wrangle?"

Michael smiled as he started to turn away. "You'll love it, Vassily; trust me."

There were no friendly forces—German, Chinese or otherwise—any closer than the perimeter of the First Chinese City. It was a stall for time and the chance to survive. Despite the fact he had lied, Michael Rourke somehow felt his father would have been proud of him—if he lived long enough that his father would ever find out.

"Han! I need you and one other man! Otto would be best!" He kept walking as, from behind him, he heard Prokopiev shouting up into the Soviet position.

There was always some means by which to cheat death, his father had taught him and his sister, always some means to trick fate, if you had the mental agility to conceive it and the nerve to attempt it.

Already, his mind was racing. He heard answering shouts in Russian from the rocks on both sides of the gap. He assumed that Major Vassily Mikhailovitch Prokopiev was shouting his commands rather than using the radio set Michael had observed attached to Prokopiev's helmet as a gesture of good faith. But was Prokopiev perhaps whispering into his headset? There was no way to know at all.

If he could get Han and Otto out on horseback, ostensibly going for help—Michael Rourke felt the corners of his mouth raising in a smile.

There might, indeed, be a way to sidestep what seemed inevitable.

As Otto and Han came forward out of the rocks, Michael signaled them toward where the Pryzwalski-like horses were still grazing. He walked quickly, but evenly, so as to avoid frightening the creatures away. After a moment, Han and Otto were flanking him. "What did you say to that Russian major?" Hammerschmidt asked under his breath.

"We formed a temporary alliance against a Maoist army that's about two hours away. Two of his men will go to rendezvous with their extraction unit—at least I think so. You two are supposed to rendezvous with the German-Chinese army that my father's leading."

"What army?" Otto Hammerschmidt exclaimed incredulously, his accent showing stronger than it usually did.

"This is insane!" Han Lu Chen murmured.

"No shit," Michael agreed. "We know my father's in Georgia and the nearest friendly forces are all the way back at the First City. He doesn't, evidently. If he's a man of his word, which I doubt, then we can rely on the agreement we made of mutual safe conduct whosever reinforcements arrive first. Assuming the contrary, it'll be up to you guys to bail me and the rest of your men out."

"How?" Han asked.

They were nearing the horses, the two Russians coming down from the rocks to join their commander, the other Russians who had been in position above the overhang on the western side of the gap, fully visible now as they crossed the long way down toward the gaps at the far end at the bottleneck there. It would be easier to ambush forces coming from that direction.

There was little time, Michael reaching for his own horse first, the ill-tempered creature nipping at his hand, missing, as he grabbed the bridle tight in his fists. "Ride out—well enough away that you won't be detected even with binoculars from the eastern wall. Then you'll have to circle back the long way so you won't be spotted. I'll be up on the western wall with the rest of our guys. The Russians'll be on the east wall. You'll have to come up behind them. We'll have to gamble on using the radios, that they won't pick up our frequency. Then we go for getting them in a crossfire if it comes to that. I don't like this—" Michael Rourke's stomach churned at thoughts of such duplicity, but the Russians would do worse, he told himself. But, would they? "I don't like it but we don't have any choice. Just get back as fast as you can without being detected and we'll play it by ear. That's all we can do. And hope you beat that Maoist force here. Otherwise, we're all up the creek."

"The creek?" Han Lu Chen repeated quizzically.

"It's a narrow, flowing body of water. In this case, it's brown and sticky and it smells like human excrement.

And we'll be up to our eyeballs in it if this doesn't work," he grinned. Otto was the poorest of them with horses, and he passed over the reins from his own horse, more subdued now, to the German commando captain, Han doing the same with another of the animals, the Russians joining them now. "Vassily — get your guys to help keep these animals under control while we get the others. Come on and give us a hand."

Prokopiev grunted something and reached for one of the animals, almost losing a finger for his trouble, then swore in Russian.

CHAPTER SEVENTEEN

Doctor Munchen was back at Iceland Base, and John Rourke had powered up the radio transceiver, now waited listening to the static as Munchen was called to the receiver. Over the crackle of static, the familiar voice came back at last. "Munchen here. Over."

"This is John Rourke, Doctor. I'm sorry to get you out of bed. Over."

"It is always a pleasure to speak with you, Herr Doctor Rourke. How may I assist? Over."

"I need a frank answer to a very frank question. And I have no choice but to trust your response, Doctor. Over."

There was a moment's pause, the static increasing, then subsiding as Munchen's voice returned. "Go ahead. Over."

"Since this transmission could be monitored, there should be no purpose in clearing the room, but if you wish, I'll wait. Over."

Another pause, then, "As you say, Herr Doctor, this transmission might well be monitored, if only by accident. Pray ask. Over."

John Rourke looked at his daughter, his friend, Paul Rubenstein, at Akiro Kurinami and Elaine Halversen. They virtually ringed him as he sat before the radio transceiver which had been given to him by the Germans in the first place. "This is a difficult question,

Doctor Munchen. Is there an active Nazi under-ground movement of which you are aware which might be working for the violent overthrow of Deiter Bern's government? Over."

The band was dead for several moments, all except for the crackle of static.

"I cannot talk concerning this over an unrestricted frequency, Herr Doctor. Nor, under the present cir-cumstances. Over."

John Rourke smiled. Munchen had answered his question. He imagined that Munchen would be smil-ing as well. "I understand, Doctor Munchen. I'll look forward to discussing this at greater length sometime in the future should circumstances permit. Now, go back to bed. Rourke out."

"And you the same, Herr Doctor. Munchen out."

John Rourke clicked off.

"That's as definite an answer as I could have hoped for," he told Annie, Paul, Akiro and Elaine. "It answers our question. Annie—get on the radio to the German base outside Eden Base. Call in for a chopper if they can risk getting one up or a J-7V to pick us up at the base of the mountain." And John Rourke looked at Kurinami and Halversen. "All of us, if you're willing to take the gamble. Because Dodd knows the location of the Retreat and he'll just send someone else after you if you stay behind. I don't think any of the explo-sives they had with them could have burst through enough granite to penetrate the Retreat. And while Annie's making that radio call, Paul—you and I are going to put more insulation behind those escape tun-nel doors. Akiro—if you'd give us a hand, we'd appre-ciate it. Next time they run a thermal scan, they won't find anything. I should have thought of that when I originally built this," and Rourke's hands gestured sweepingly over the Retreat.

Kurinami looked at Elaine Halversen, then at Rourke. "What about Commander Dodd?"

"He won't dare do anything openly with me there, and we might be able to force him to back off just by going to Eden Base. We know his secret. So, he'll want all of us dead as quickly as he can get it done, but not openly, not officially, because this Nazi thing could ruin him. And he knows it. Well?"

Kurinami looked at Elaine Halversen again. She put her hand in his, Rourke judging the gesture as at once physical and symbolic. Akiro Kurinami looked into John Rourke's eyes. "We will go."

"Good man," John Rourke nodded, clapping Kurinami's shoulder.

CHAPTER EIGHTEEN

Nicolai Antonovitch had excelled in tactics, but he had also learned that the obvious was too easily ignored; and now, as a commander, tactics were his to suggest, strategy his to determine. He had listened to the battle plans of his field commanders as they sat about the hermetically sealed, environmentally controlled tent, the Mongolian winds howling outside, but this something he knew only because he had ventured out earlier and he had consulted the long range weather forecast.

The yellow cast of the overhead lights made the green chalkboards appear almost gray. He stood, merely to stretch himself, and all of his field commanders watched him as though he were about to do something important. He was beginning, more and more, to appreciate how being the supreme commander could convince a man that he was also a god. It had done so to the Hero Marshal, the Hero Egotist. Colonel Nicolai Antonovitch had vowed to himself from the first that it would not do so to him.

He meandered about the enclosure, listening as battle plans were discussed, dissected, determined. And at last, when all his field commanders except Prokopiev (who was late for his helicopter rendezvous after the reconnaissance mission to the Second Chinese City) had spoken, Antonovitch quietly cleared his throat in preparation of speaking. But the clearing of his throat silenced the assembled officers as though a bell had been rung or a horn blown. All eyes turned to him.

He cleared his throat again, considered just sitting down and letting the discussions work their interminable way to a conclusion. But there was no time for games.

"Comrades. We must consider the overall strategy now," Antonovitch began. All eyes were his still. "Our allied enemies will never anticipate a move so daring in scope, because they would view it as foolhardy, which if it were to fail, indeed, it would be. But we must risk all, or at least appear to do so. Our allied enemies know nothing of our normalization of relations with the Underground City, and therefore grossly underestimate our strength and our abilities to re-supply. Until tonight, none of you knew the overall strategy, but as each of you has revealed his battle plans, it will have become clear that we are about to engage in a three-pronged attack."

With that, Antonovitch walked to the blackboard and reached over it to the mounted chart rollers, drawing down the central of three charts. It was a Van der Grinten Projection of the World.

On the map were three red stars, one over the location of the Second Chinese City, one over the Hekla Community of Lydveldid Island, the third over Eden Base in south central American Georgia which had once been the United States. "Simultaneously," he began again, gesturing to each red star placement one after the other, "we shall strike these three targets. With such rapidity shall we strike that there shall not be time or personnel for our allied enemies to react, let alone prevent our success. Here—" and he gestured to American Georgia "—we shall strike against Eden Base and the German installation which guards it. Airborne elements will attack the German base and neutralize radar and other sensing equipment, while helicopter gunships move in to destroy Eden Base. The goal is to take the objective while maintaining destruction of the installation's extensive runway facilities and technological capabilities below the level of thirty-five per cent. Meanwhile," and Antonovitch shifted his hand toward Hekla community, "our troops shall attack the German installation which guards Hekla community, utilizing the same general plan. That is to say that airborne forces will penetrate the base, destroy advanced warning systems and open the door for a helicopter gunship force to attack Hekla community itself. But, unlike the assault in American Georgia, the goal is total destruction of the German installation and total chaos in the Hekla community. With the base in American Georgia under our control, the base in Lydveldid Island will be insupportable and abandoned."

Antonovitch watched the eyes of his officers. There was admiration there. The godhood thing. He shrugged it away. His hand moved to the third objective. "Here, at the Second Chinese City, totally different tactics will be employed," Antonovitch hoped, because all his plans for the Chinese objective rested on the successful on-site reconnaissance of the

Second Chinese City by Prokopiev's Elite Corps unit. "Here," he began again, "the Elite Corps will parachute in and attack the city from the ground, striking boldly—" he was improvising generalities as he proceeded "—to the heart of the Second City government, seizing control of communications, power and other facilities, demanding surrender." His hand drifted over the portion of Western Eruope where, at one time, there had been the country of France. "On the return from Hekla community, our forces will strike at the small German installation in the area bordering the lands to where the Wild Tribes were relocated. Unlike my predecessor, I have no thirst for genocide." Some eyebrows were raised at his words, but he made no attempt to recant.

"The goal in attacking this secondary objective," Antonovitch continued quickly, "is to further disrupt German lines of command and supply. There will be no attempt to attack the areas where the Wild Tribes are living, nor will the pre-fabricated factories which have begun servicing their needs for food and shelter be attacked. If the German technicians care to continue their work after the installation and the runways are destroyed, so be it. The area is of a humanitarian nature and therefore not a fit military target for the people of the Soviet. This raid will be carried out quickly. Our troops will re-equip at the Underground City, then proceed at best speed to reinforce our personnel at the Second Chinese City and hold this position against the inevitable attack from the First Chinese City."

His eyes traveled over the room again. "The German units in Asia will be cut off and forced to surrender or die. The only serious German force will be baseless outside its homeland. As conditions permit, once our new territories have been secured, the new German homeland in what was Argentina can be assaulted and destroyed should its masters fail to realize the inevitability of their fate and surrender. And the Rourkes, of course, will be without help. They will, inevitably, be captured and made to stand trial for their offenses, or killed. And, in the final analysis, the death of the Hero Marshal shall be forever avenged." And there would be peace, and the earth could once again flourish and, with control of the nuclear weapons the leadership of the Second Chinese City could lead him to, that peace would be enforceable.

He had read of the Pax Romana, the world peace achieved through military conquest. It was, in this case, the only way for the planet to step out of the dark ages of warfare into which, as the Americans had called it, the Night of the War had thrust mankind.

Whether this was the goal of the leadership of the Underground City or not mattered little to him. If their minds were like, then let them run this new world he would give them. If their goals were other than his, they would be powerless to stop him.

If he trusted anyone that thoroughly, he would have confided that the death of the Hero Marshal might one day be looked upon as one of the singularly greatest moments in human history, for Karamatsov would have destroyed the earth.

To rule among the ashes, to be master of the dead and dying, to know that in the end all would have been for nothing, seemed senseless, seemed mad to him.

"So, Comrades. What questions do you have? Because, Comrades, we strike—" and he consulted the Breitling watch at his left wrist "—we strike in fewer than twenty-four hours. And we shall forever alter the course of the future. Questions?"

There were none.

CHAPTER NINETEEN

The Chinese heavy cavalry were upon them before they realized, and before a radio transmission came in from Han Lu Chen and Otto Hammerschmidt.

With a radio headset provided to him by his ally Major Vassily Mikhailovitch Prokopiev, so resistance to the Maoist forces could be coordinated, Prokopiev had said in panicked sounding English, "They come!"

From his side of the gap, Michael had been unable to see, and the wind had risen, so as dark gray—so dark they were almost black—clouds had driven in from the west that he had been unable to hear.

"They're coming!" Michael rasped with a loud stage whisper, the Russian medical corpsman still on his side of the gap, attending the injured, most seriously wounded among them one of the Chinese enlisted men, the few survivors clustered around Michael Rourke as he waited for Prokopiev to open fire.

The Maoist cavalry was broken up into two distinct units, men dressed in the furs and astrakhan hats and informal body armor of the Mongol mercenaries, looking for all the world like something out of a Hollywood epic from centuries ago, and (the larger element of the mounted force) men in faded pale red battle dress utilities, gray military looking parkas and baseball caps. Even the mounts of what Michael Rourke assumed to be regular army as opposed to mercenary, were less spectacular, all a dun brown or bay, not the gleaming blacks and speckled appaloosa-like mounts of the Mongols. Some of the Mongol horses, as opposed to the mounts of the regulars, were not the Pryzwalski-like animals so common here, but instead larger bod-ied, broad faced animals with powerful, sinewy necks and several hands taller as well, looking clearly to have Arabian lineage. Despite the natural independence of the breed, Michael Rourke felt these animals would be worth the challenge of a hard ride. He wondered if he would have the chance.

The buttstock of the M-16 was checked tight to his face, his right eye blinking periodically to keep from losing sight picture. He had taken aim on the evident commander of the force, a wizened-looking man of perhaps seventy, but tall, once a formidable figure, as Michael judged it. From the braid which adorned his baseball cap, Michale judged him at least a field grade officer if not higher. But it was the philosophy of the old cowboys and Indians movies he had watched as a boy at the Retreat. Shoot the chief and, while the enemy was disorganized, make your play.

He was ready to shoot the chief.

"That old man is a general, I think," Prokopiev's voice hissed in his ear through the headset.

"I've got him Vassily."

"No—we will need this man if there is to be any hope of forcing them back. Trust this."

"You and I apparently grew up on different movies. John Wayne would have shot the guy."

"John Wayne?"

"A great actor, and in his way an ambassador of American moral values and philosophy."

"I see. Do not shoot the old officer."

"Fine—shut up, will ya, so I can shoot something?"

Michael Rourke took a last glance at the old man, then shifted his rifle to another target, a younger officer. Prokopiev was the professional military man, Michael Rourke told himself.

The rattle of sabers, the clattering of sling swivels, the clopping of hooves was louder now than the wind.

Michael settled his sights easily over the younger officer's chest.

Like an evil angel on his shoulder, Vassily Prokopiev's voice came again. "On the count of three. One—" Michael Rourke suddenly asked himself why he was listening to this man at all. After all, Prokopiev had engineered the miserably failed ambush which had trapped him and the others here but achieved no military purpose. What was to imply that Prokopiev could do better now. "Two—" If it could be avoided, if they survived this, he would be just as content to leave Prokopiev to fight another day, and he would do all that was possible to ensure that. The duplicity he intended rankled him, but there was no other way for it. Where was Han? Where was Otto?

"Three—now!"

Michael Rourke touched his finger to the M-16's trigger a micro-second after the first shot of the first burst began, and as the Maoist officer rocked back and tumbled from the back of his rat-like horse, others falling around him, bloodcurdling screams issuing from the Mongrol mercenaries, Michael Rourke almost said aloud, "So much for diplomacy."

CHAPTER TWENTY

The struggle down the mountainside had been difficult, but most difficult on the women. Annie, of course, was in excellent physical condition, but Elaine Halversen's stamina could best be described as better than average, Paul thought, realizing that at times his thinking was becoming as clinical as that of a Rourke. He charted it off to propinquity and good fortune.

But, as the pilot of the J-7V had recounted and landing at the German installation outside Eden Base had confirmed, good fortune was something they all shared. Fresh from New Germany in Argentina, come to personally investigate the situation involving Kurinami and Halversen, was Colonel Wolfgang Mann, supreme military commander of New Germany, a man whom Paul Rubenstein at once trusted and deeply respected.

They were shown to quarters, Kurinami and Halversen asked if they would prefer to share quarters (they had preferred) and then a breakfast meeting was announced with Colonel Mann.

Paul showered with Annie, letting her massage the tenseness from his neck and back and upper arms, and, despite the precious little sleep they had been allowed, after they dried each other, they made slow, comfortable love, after which Annie had fallen asleep in his arms and he in hers.

A quick shower and breakfast awaited them, Annie dressed in long skirt and lace trimmed blouse of Icelandic fashion. He had asked, when they had packed their gear for the expedition to the Retreat, why she had elected to waste precious ounces on things so seemingly patently unnecessary as a skirt and petticoat and a fancy blouse and she had told him simply, "If you were a woman, you'd understand. But I'm considering that you don't."

And he was convinced now, as he tasted the ground beef patties served so obviously instead of pork-based sausage (a German favorite, he had learned) in deference to his religion, that Annie could read his mind. Because his thoughts were consumed with her, he saw her watching him, smiling, almost blushing as he had recollected what they had done with each other's bodies early in the morning hours before they had slept.

He forced his attention to his food and the conversation around him, and just in time because Colonel Mann began to address him. "So, Herr Rubenstein. It is satisfactory? The food?"

"Yes — and thank you for your consideration, Colonel."

"It is nothing, Herr Rubenstein. But you are gracious to notice it. And, I assure you, all is, to the best of our abilities here, how do you say it?"

"Kosher?" Paul smiled.

"Indeed," Mann smiled back.

Paul Rubenstein doubted the beef was exactly Kosher, but it would serve. "And Frau Rubenstein," Mann continued. "You are lovelier than ever. Marriage indeed must agree with you."

144

"Thank you, Colonel Mann. And how is your lovely wife?"

"She is in excellent health and I am certain will be furious that an opportunity to meet with so many members of the Rourke family at once has been missed. But—" And he raised his hands, palms upward, in a gesture of resignation.

Mann looked at Elaine Halversen, who sat across the table from him. "Doctor Halversen. Although I know little beyond official reports of the nature of the difficulties which seem to beset you and Lieutenant Kurinami, I assure you that I will do all that is within my power that they be alleviated."

John Rourke spoke. "This is sensitive, Colonel. Do you wish the attendants to leave? I'm sure we can pour our own coffee and the ladies might be prevailed upon to help us if we get in trouble passing the eggs or the toast."

Paul Rubenstein watched as John's and Colonel Mann's eyes met. "Yes. A fine suggestion, Herr Doctor." And without looking at the enlisted personnel who had served the breakfast, he spoke a few words in German, dismissing them. He looked at John, saying, "More orange juice, Herr Doctor? Frozen from concentrate, the oranges grown in our own groves, as you know."

"Yes—"

"Here—let me," and Annie was already up before Paul could reach for her chair, taking the orange juice pitcher. "Elaine—help me with the coffee? Hmm?"

Elaine Halversen nodded, stood, Kurinami getting her chair, and she took one of the coffee pots off the

145

table and began filling cups. The coffee was freshly ground and Paul Rubenstein had decided that he would drink it until he felt he would float.

"This sensitive matter, Herr Doctor?"

"Yes."

"Ladies — may I smoke?" Mann interjected.

Elaine merely nodded, Annie saying, "Certainly," and as Colonel Mann took out a cigarette, he offered them to John, John taking one. Annie snatched her father's lighter off the table from beside him and lit the cigarette for him. Times like this, Paul Rubenstein wished he had never quit.

"Thanks, sweetheart," John told Annie, then as he exhaled, he addressed Wolfgang Mann. "Colonel, I have reason to believe that there is a conspiracy, of which you are already aware, among supporters of the deposed Nazi leadership, to forcibly overthrow your current government under Deiter Bern. I have evidence to support that some such persons as were involved in this conspiracy were acting in complicity with Commander Christopher Dodd, the de facto leader of Eden Base. Their overall purpose is unclear, but I assume it has to do with utilizing Eden as a legitimate front for their revolutionary activities. Eight men — whom Paul and I dispatched with some assistance — were in the process of attacking the Retreat, my mountain home, in order to presumably kill Lieutenant Kurinami and his fiance, Doctor Halversen, who were my guests. They were, by all appearances, German, and they utilized a mixture of German and U.S. small arms, along with a German manufactured disposable rocket launcher which, though delivering an extremely powerful explosive

146

device, I would assume is not currently inventoried."

"The R-19 MK II?"

"Why? Are you missing some?" John Rourke smiled.

"As a matter of fact, I am."

"Well, consider sixteen of the missing articles accounted for, then."

"That leaves approximately four hundred and eighty remaining."

Paul Rubenstein began to cough, a piece of ground beef sticking in his throat. He washed it down with a quickly gulped swallow of orange juice. Wolfgang Mann laughed as he turned to look at him. "Indeed, Herr Rubenstein, it is a serious matter." Mann looked back to John Rourke. "Did you get any names?"

"The men involved, as I indicated, are no longer available for questioning. But Paul and I heard one of the men call another of them by the name 'Weil' and another called 'Horst'."

"The one was Hans Weil, the other I would need to consult intelligence files for. Hans Weil was once a German officer. He was also a Nazi. He was never found after the victory against the leader and Deiter Bern's taking charge of the government. At least, it appears, he is accounted for. He was SS."

"How many more are there like him?" Annie asked suddenly.

Wolfgang Mann looked at her as he tapped ashes from his cigarette, "Regrettably, Frau Rubenstein, several hundred that we know of. There may be hundreds of others who openly profess distaste for the old regime yet would support it were it to return. National Socialism dies hard. There are some who think it never dies." He looked at John Rourke. "And these men were attempting to penetrate your mountain Retreat in order to kill Doctor Halversen and Lieutenant Kurinami?"

"Yes, Colonel. At the order of Commander Dodd, most likely, with his complicity almost certainly. I am asking that Akiro and Elaine be given sanctuary here, regardless of Dodd's wishes or demands. Arrest them, if you like, on some charge or another so you can hold them in custody if diplomacy will best be served. But don't return them to Dodd. Otherwise, they'll be killed through some contrivance or another. I think we both know that."

"Why do you think I came, Herr Doctor? Because I enjoy this rather disappointing climate?"

John Rourke laughed, a hearty, genuine laugh. "I have your assurances, then?"

"Yes. And I would like to have your help, Herr Doctor. I must unearth the leaders of this conspiracy against the Fatherland, and I imagine you would be equally interested in bringing Commander Dodd to book."

"Before the discoveries I learned of at Mid-Wake, as I wrote you by dispatch and as Doctor Munchen's accounts have no doubt reinforced, I was firmly convinced that the best method for destroying a cancer was, if all else proved inadequate, excision. I have since learned of subtler methods; but it is, after all, the end result which is important."

Paul Rubenstein, at times, felt like John H. Watson, despite the fact that his weight was all wrong for the part.

148

Annie poured him more coffee and smiled at him, her hand brushing against his, her Sherlockian father continuing to speak. "Michael, my son, has gone off to the Second Chinese City. Before attempting to solve this Dodd matter, if you'll indulge me, I'd like to get back to China. We still have a substantial lack of meaningful intelligence concerning Karamatsov's forces and who is running the show in his place, and I'd like to be nearby just in case Michael's embassy—"

"A peace mission, Herr Doctor? Yes—to the Second Chinese City. I recall it was to be undertaken. There is so much happening."

"Agreed. But Hartman is monitoring the movements of the Soviet army and the events at the Underground City. He's spread a bit thin. If something should go wrong with Michael's mission, I want to be close enough to act."

"My best wishes, then, of course," Mann nodded, lighting another cigarette after offering one—accepted—to John Rourke. Rourke lit his own and the colonel's. "I would relieve Hartman's command were it possible, but with maintaining bases here and in Iceland and in what was France and Hartman's existing force to monitor the Soviets, I am severely undermanned at New Germany. Were the Russians to strike there in force, we would be hard pressed to repel them."

"I understand. And the last thing you need is an enemy within. I'll get back to Eden Base as soon as practical. I'd ask Paul to volunteer, or Annie for that matter, but if I'm needed, we'll all be needed."

"Agreed. Agreed. Yes."

149

"What will happen when Dodd learns we're here?" Elaine Halversen asked suddenly, her face gray tinged.

"We will be fine," Kurinami assured her.

"Indeed you will. But we may find out shortly," Mann smiled. "I instructed that he be informed the moment you arrived. Since I have little use for Commander Dodd, I thought it only fitting that he be awakened from a peaceful sleep by news of your arrival. So far, he has done nothing. But the morning is still young. And, I assure you, you and your lieutenant shall be afforded the full and considerable protection of New Germany, Fraulein Doctor. That is my pledge."

John Rourke raised his coffee cup. "Let's drink to that, then!" And even Elaine Halversen smiled.

CHAPTER TWENTY-ONE

The Mongol mercenaries were without fear of death, Michael Rourke realized. They forced their mounts with whips and sabers up into the higher rocks, the animals slipping and skidding under them, blood on the animals from where they'd been beaten sometimes visible in a reflected streak of light from an accidentally burnished piece of armor or the flash of a blade. Although the armor seemed more ceremonial, like a costume, than to serve a practical purpose, no single burst from an M-16 would put one of them down.

Michael Rourke's rifle was fired out, no time to change magazines as three of the Mongols who had whipped and heeled their horses almost vertically along the rock face neared him. He let the rifle fall to his side on its sling and tore the twin Beretta pistols from their holsters under his armpits beneath his parka, firing them almost point blank at the charging enemy mercenaries, one of the men down, another wounded or simply unhorsed as his animal stumbled, horse and man skidding back along the gray rock surface toward the floor of the gap, the third man's horse jumping the lip of the rocks from behind which Michael and his meager force and the Soviet medical corpsman fought, Michael sidestepping as the man's saber wheeled toward him, the animal under him rearing, a pistol firing simultaneously, the rock beside

Michael's feet disintegrating. Michael safed both 92F Berettas and crossdrew his knife from the sheath at his left hip, throwing his body weight against the legs of the Mongol's mount, his body shuddering with the impact.

The horse—one of the larger animals clearly of Arabian lineage—stumbled, fell, the man spilling from the saddle, the pistol flying from his hand as his body impacted the ground, the saber still bunched tight in his fingerless-gloved fist. Michael went for him with the knife old Jan the Icelandic swordmaker had crafted for him after the centuries old pattern of the Life Support System II.

Steel locked to steel, the saber of the Mongol vastly longer, but the knife in Michael Rourke's right fist he felt was stronger. Michael's body weight hammered the Mongol back even as he rose, forcing him to his knees; their blades were still crossed.

The Mongol snarled something unintelligible, the smell of his breath overpoweringly bad as it hissed through the yellowed stumps of his teeth, their faces inches apart. The Mongol drew a small, curved blade knife, Michael's left hand catching the left wrist, the knife at crotch level as they pushed against one another, each trying to overpower the other's balance, Michael's legs pistoning against the Mongol's superior body weight.

Michael drew back, loosing the knife hand, the steel of Michael's knife scraping against the steel of the Mongol's saber, the saber twirling in the Mongol's hand, Michael Rourke parrying the thrust as it came, their blades stroking, the Mongol charging him. Michael threw himself down and forward, under the arc of the Mongol's saber, the LS II raking across the Mongol's thighs and right kneecap as Michael rolled away and the Mongol tumbled forward to his face. Michael threw himself onto the man's back, the Mongol rearing like an unbroken animal, Michael almost thrown clear, but hammering the knife blade downward into the right kidney.

The Mongol shrieked what had to be a curse, Michael's legs binding around him at the hips now, the Mongol tumbling forward as Michael Rourke wrenched his blade clear, then thrust it into the throat, the shriek dying almost as soon as it had begun.

Michael Rourke staggered to his feet, in his mind for a moment seeing it as if it had only just happened, the man in the rumpled clothes who had come into the barn and was trying to make Michael's mother fellate him, Michael seeing his own hand as it clenched over the catspaw-surfaced boning knife they had taken with them from the kitchen in the house they had abandoned the night before when the bombing came.

And then Michael's conscious will was no longer involved, and the knife moved in his hand and into the evil man's right kidney and the man screamed and died and his mother cried and held him.

Michael Rourke was just standing there, bullets impacting the rocks around him. His knife was still in his right fist, and he wiped it clean of blood on the dead Mongol's body. As he sheathed the knife, he threw himself down out of the line of fire, his rifle tossed to him by the Soviet medical corpsman, more of the Mongols charging up the steep sides of the

153

gap, regular troops kneeling beside their mounts, firing up into the rocks, the Mongols firing from the saddle as they rode, and with greater accuracy.

Michael rammed a fresh magazine up the M-16's well, firing into a knot of the Mongols as they urged their horses up the rock wall, two of the Mongols going down, their horses with them. Michael could see the Soviet position on the other side of the gap, his radio headset lost in the fight with the Mongol a moment earlier. There was fighting there, hand to hand.

He heard one of the Chinese from the First City — the nearly dying trooper — shouting, screaming. Michael swung around, two of the Mongols and a regular Maoist officer charging down on the man, somehow having circled around them from behind. Michael fired out the M-16, cutting down the Maoist officer and one of the Mongols, then throwing down his empty rifle, both of the partially spent Beretta pistols coming into his hands, firing, the second Mongol stumbling back as his saber half-cleaved the First City trooper's head from his neck, arterial blood spurting geyser-like into the wind.

Michael fired again, a double tap from each pistol, the Mongol's body spinning, falling to the ground.

There was a shout from beside him, Michael wheeling toward the sound. The Soviet medical corpsman was using his empty rifle like a club, trying to fend off two Mongols with sabers. Michael Rourke shot one of the men, but both pistols were empty now. As the Soviet medic tried for a momentary advantage with the Mongol, the Mongol's saber cleaved him almost in two, hacking downward where

154

the neck met the right shoulder and into the chest, a hideous scream from the dying Russian.

Michael Rourke's right hand found the butt of the .44 Magnum revolver and he stabbed it toward the Mongol, firing, the slug ripping through the Mongol's wide open mouth, yellowed teeth exploding outward on both sides of the mouth, the head snapping back into a cloud of gore which sprayed from the exit wound.

Michael turned toward the rocks across which more of the Mongols were coming. A Mongol horseman, his saber flying. Michael shot him from the saddle, a second Mongol's saber crashing down, Michael wheeling toward the man to fire, the saber coming as he backstepped, a blinding explosion of light and more pain in his head than he had ever known, and then darkness.

CHAPTER TWENTY-TWO

The young pilot named Lintz sat at the controls of the same J-7V. "Did you get to radio your wife, Olga?"

"Yes, Herr Doctor. And she misses me so," he smiled.

John Rourke was about to reply when Annie, sitting toward the rear of the plane, asleep the last Rourke had noticed, screamed.

Rourke punched the safety restraint's quick release and was up, moving along the fuselage, Annie screaming again, Paul kneeling beside her, arms around her. Annie's brown eyes opened wide. "It's Michael—Paul, daddy—it's Michael. I saw it!" And she screamed, but as if she were in terrible pain, her hands going to cover her eyes.

Rourke dropped to his knees before her, beside her husband. "Annie—Annie!"

She screamed, cried. "Ann Rourke Rubenstein! Stop it!" Rourke shouted to his daughter, his hands on her shoulders, shaking her.

Her hands came down from her eyes. She sniffed back a tear. "Daddy!"

John Rourke folded his daughter into his arms. "Tell me what you saw," he almost whispered.

"It was something like a sword and it caught in the light and there was an explosion, but it was inside Michael's head and I felt it—daddy!"

"It's all right, baby," Rourke cooed to her, rocking her in his arms. His eyes met Paul's, and he moved his daughter out of his own arms into Paul's arms, then rested back on his haunches.

His daughter had not been born with a gift; it was a curse in the truest sense of the word.

John Rourke closed his eyes.

CHAPTER TWENTY-THREE

They had stopped for refueling at the base outside Hekla community and, as a courtesy, although he could barely concentrate on the few words he spoke to her, he called the President of Lydveldid Island, Madame Jokli. When she asked if all were well, he told her simply that he would see.

And then the aircraft was off again, speeding across the now deserted British Isles, making radio contact with the smallish base in France where there was a small German installation to assist the relocated people of the Wild Tribes, cutting across Italy and the Adriatic and across Greece and landing in Turkey near the Bosporous where a small German garrison held a synth-fuel station and then airborne again, toward China.

Once Annie had calmed down sufficiently, he administered a sedative by injection, letting her fall asleep in Paul's arms, then helping Paul to cover her with a blanket, the effect of the sedative worn off by now, her breathing even, regular, her sleep natural. That she seemed totally dreamless chilled John Rourke more than if she had been actively dreaming, restless. Was she no longer experiencing Michael's assumed plight because Michael was safe? Or was he dead.

Rourke lit the thin, dark tobacco cigar that had been clenched tight in his teeth unlit for the past several minutes, rolling the battered Zippo's striking wheel under his thumb. The German flints he used lasted longer than any flints he had ever used. He studied the lighter in his hands for a moment, turning it over, his initials — J.T.R. — drawing his attention. He had always wanted for his children — like any parent — that they should live in happiness and peace. Michael — if he still lived — had been widowed, his wife of so little time, Madison, and the unborn child she carried murdered in one of the Soviet terror raids on Helka. And Annie. The ability to see what logic dictated could not be seen, to invade the thoughts of others. Her abilities — extra-sensory, psychic, paranormal, whatever the term — seemed only to increase. And he had noticed the faintest beginnings of such abilities in his son, although he doubted they would ever even approach the magnitude of hers. Was it the effect of the Sleep on their young minds, or was it simply something that would have surfaced regardless of circumstance? John Rourke doubted the latter. He exhaled smoke through his nostrils, pocketing the lighter.

After first becoming aware of Annie's abilities, Doctor Munchen had asked for the opportunity of testing them, first calling for Rourke and Paul Rubenstein, asking permission of father and husband before asking hers. Paul had looked at him — Rourke — and John Rourke had lowered his eyes toward Paul. Paul cleared his throat. "I don't like this stuff, Doctor Munchen. But this is Annie's life, and she'll make the decision. Thanks for consulting us, but it wasn't necessary."

And then Munchen had asked Annie. She had

asked Paul. She had gone ahead with the tests. Using standard tests, largely unchanged from the days in medical school when some of Rourke's fellow students had played with the cards, tested each other's responses, Annie had passed faultlessly. There was not a star nor a triangle nor a wavy line she could not read through the back of the card. There was not a sealed envelope, the contents of which were known to Munchen, that when she tried to read Munchen the contents remained secret.

But she almost never tried, because, as she had told Munchen when he — Rourke — and Paul had been called in midway during the tests, she was frightened of this ability.

It was the dreams which most terrified John Rourke. She would see danger, feel it, almost experience it. It was such a dream which had caused her to hasten the time of the Awakening when she had known Michael was in danger for his life.

And now — John Rourke studied the glowing tip of his cigar.

Then Annie screamed as though someone had driven a knife into her breast, her body rigid with pain as he reached her, eyes dilated with fear — but for none of it was there a physical cause. "Michael!"

CHAPTER TWENTY-FOUR

Michael Rourke's eyes felt as though they were on fire and simultaneously coated with salt, his entire body consumed with more pain than he had ever known, as if the pain from the sword blow had never ended, was eternal.

His vision was blurred and his muscles were cramped and through the blur when he again forced his eyes to open, he could see Prokopiev, the right side of Prokopiev's face covered in blood.

Michael started to turn his head—and the pain drove consciousness from him . . . As he raised his head, the pain returned and when his eyes opened he could not fully part the lids. He moved his hands and the muscles in his neck and shoulders cried out to him and he stopped moving, fighting to remain conscious. Slowly, moving as little as possible, his hands reached his face and his eyes were all but crusted over. As gently as he could, his fingers swollen and stiff, he pulled at the scabs of blood until his right eye opened. His vision cleared after a few seconds.

He began to work at the left eye, the result the same, but there was terrible pain in his left temple.

With his restored vision (he could not yet move his head), he watched Vassily Prokopiev, the Russian commander appearing more dead than alive and unmoved since Michael had last looked at him—how long ago? His wristwatch—he did not move his head after the first unconscious attempt had brought the pain washing over him again—and so he felt for it. The Rolex was gone.

The Mongols.

He shivered and when the cold washed over him, the pain increased and he looked at his feet. Shackles were about his bare ankles, his boots and socks gone.

"Proko—Prokopiev," he called out feebly.

The Russian commander was alive at least. He muttered something incomprehensible but did not move. "Prokopiev—Vassily Prokopiev!"

Prokopiev's head moved slightly, then sagged down to his chest.

Michael fought to keep focus. Prokopiev, as well, was bootless, ankles shackled. But they had left him his socks. Prokopiev's BDU jacket was gone, the pistol belt gone too, Prokopiev's black sweater half ripped from his upper body and bloodstains visibly along his neck.

Slowly, so he would not pass out again, Michael Rourke began to move his head, to the right.

Another Russian, the face blue veined and livid, the ankles shackled, dead on the almost black stone floor less than two yards away. Another Russian still, a crude bandage over his naked chest, the bandage saturated dark red with blood, ankles shackled, Michael was suddenly aware of the sound of the Russian's labored breathing.

Michael arced his head left, slowly, seeing the dead man again, seeing Prokopiev again, his head and eyes stopping as he reached the heavy steel door a yard from him.

He was tempted to shout, if his voice still worked well enough for that. It had sounded strained and felt dry as he had called out to Prokopiev. But he did not shout, instead returning his gaze to Prokopiev.

Michael Rourke closed his eyes then and began to focus on what had to be done. The still living, seriously wounded Russian. Check the chest wound, see if the bleeding has stopped. He reminded himself that was contingent on whether or not he could walk or crawl, or for that matter whether or not the shackles on his ankles were somehow fastened to the wall against which he leaned.

He tried raising his left hand, to inspect the wound to his head from the sword blow. When the stiffened fingers of his left hand found the wound the pain washed over him suddenly, consumed him . . . Michael Rourke opened his eyes, this time without great difficulty. They were not crusted over and he presumed the bleeding had stopped. He was colder than he had been, but he was aware of a throbbing pain on the left side of his head near the crown of the skull, which, he theorized, meant that his overall pain level had reduced.

Slowly, he moved his head, raising it, leaning his head back against the damp stone of the wall against which he reclined. The chamber's ceiling seemed at least a dozen feet above him, but that could have been perspective. He would know better when he stood. But first the shackles. He lowered his head, pain washing over him, but consciousness not ebbing. He visually inspected the shackles. They were steel, the chain links seeming sturdy, but the shackles were not attached to any chain leading to the wall. The distance between the shackles was perhaps eighteen inches, which would make walking difficult, if he could stand.

And his balance would be impeded by them, of course, Michael reminded himself.

He tried to stand, his back twisting with the agony of movement. He fell partially forward, but kept conscious, catching himself on his hands. There was no time for the luxury of unconsciousness. He would save standing. On hands and knees, he crawled across the damp floor to Prokopiev, checking vital signs as best he could.

If there were ever an end to this, he had decided that he would go to New Germany, or perhaps to the American colony, Mid-Wake, and study medicine. Prokopiev, despite the visually poor condition, had a strong pulse and breathed regularly, if somewhat shallowly. Quickly, Michael inspected the wounds that he could readily discern. What looked like a bullet crease across the left temple. It had bled considerably because there seemed to be no other wounds to the head or face. A shoulder wound, but the collar bone did not appear broken and the bleeding had stopped all but for a trickle as Michael examined it. The right shoulder appeared to be dislocated.

While he was unconscious was the best time to try it. Michael gently laid Prokopiev flat on the floor, taking the right arm by the wrist and gradually inscribing an ever enlarging arc. There was a pop and Prokopiev's entire body seemed to tremble and a moan issued from his bloodcaked lips. Michael felt the shoulder. The dislocation was reduced. There was likely substantial muscle damage, but in time that would heal. But he needed something with which to bind the arm so it would not dislocate at the ball and socket of the shoulder joint again. He considered using a portion of Prokopiev's already tattered sweater, but thought better of it. Instead, he crawled on hands and knees to the already stiffened body of the dead Russian Elite Corpsman. He stripped off the dead man's pants, the legs of the BDU trousers long enough that he could bind both the dislocation and apply a portion of the trousers as packing to the left shoulder where there was the bullet wound.

As he set to work, he heard a scream, and at last he knew the meaning of the oft-used word "blood-curdling." It was a man but barely sounded like one, and he was in terrible pain.

Michael crawled toward the door, reaching up to the bars set at chest height, touching at them gingerly lest they were electrified, then pulling himself to a standing position, the change in circulatory pattern instantly bringing him nausea and dizziness. He swayed, leaned heavily against the door, controlled his breathing.

And he peered through the bars. Mongols. Second City Chinese regulars. And a beefy looking man, naked except for long underpants, his wrists and ankles shackled to some sort of table with crank handles attached to both top and bottom. As one of the Mongols brandished a sword in the man's face, Michael Rourke heard a curse issue from his lips, in Russian.

And then someone entered the chamber and stood

beside the table on which the Russian was secured. A woman, tall, graceful, hair as black as the night well past her waist, her slender body covered in robes of maroon cloth like velvet and decorated with gold stitched figures of dragons and griffins.

She reached to one of the crank handles on the table and suddenly moved it and the Russian shrieked with pain. Michael Rourke closed his eyes, leaning his head heavily against the bars.

Ego, humanity, all demanded that he shout, ordering them to stop torturing the man—it was a medieval rack of some sort. But logic dictated attending to the injured man with the chest wound, then trying to rouse Prokopiev.

He turned away from the bars and set about doing what had to be done, securing Prokopiev's bandaging first. The screams haunted him, and so did the woman who was causing them.

The Russian was cursing them, that much Russian Michael Rourke knew. He set to work on the man with the chest wound, on his knees again, his balance better that way, working gently in the gray light to pry away just enough of the packing that if the soldier's bleeding had stopped, he would not inadvertently re-start it. But the bleeding hadn't stopped, the pulse weak, the respiration labored, the skin colder even than it should have been considering the ambient temperature of the room—dungeon—in which they were confined. The lungs were likely filling with blood, one of them perhaps already collapsed. Using the dead man's shirt, he worked to stop the bleeding, hearing a grating sound behind him, looking back, the woman in the velvet robes standing in the door,

166

her face exquisite, except for her eyes. The lids looked like deep blue tinted shrouds.

"This man is dying," Michael Rourke said to her, not knowing if she could understand. "He needs a doctor."

"He needs death," she answered, her English well spoken but curiously accented, as though she had learned it but never heard it before.

"No—"

She snapped her fingers and one of the Mongols walked past her, drawing his saber. Michael pushed himself up, nearly tripping because of the length of chain which was between his ankles, throwing himself at the Mongol, both Michael's hands locked to the Mongol's wrist. A second Mongol and two regular guards pushed into the chamber. Michael's left knee smashed up into the first Mongol's groin, a rush of incredibly foul breath from the Mongol's mouth washing over his face. As the Mongol sagged, Michael lost his balance, unable to recover it, falling in a heap to the floor with the Mongol beside him. But Michael had the saber, raking it across the abdomen of the second Mongol.

He saw the rifle butt coming and rolled away from it, losing the saber as his head slammed against the wall and the dizziness washed over him.

The Chinese woman was barking orders and more guards, Mongol and regular, were flooding the room now.

As Michael tried to stand, one of the Mongols thrust a saber into the dying Russian soldier. Michael's hands reached out, catching the Mongol by the ankle, pulling him off balance, falling on him

167

and hammering at his face with his fists until the Mongol's eyes closed.

And then the back of Michael's head felt like it was exploding.

CHAPTER TWENTY-FIVE

John Rourke had planned ahead.

After their initial success, he had ordered several more beyond the original four built, the Germans gladly complying. The original colors had been white for the prototype left for the German engineers to play with, a dark, almost British racing green one for Natalia, a medium blue colored one for Paul Rubenstein and his own, colored like his Harley, jet black. All four of these, plus one more were waiting as the J-7V touched down and Rourke looked to the far edge of the landing field.

The German Specials. But why were there five of them rather than three. About the size of his jet black Harley Low Rider, they combined the best features of twentieth century motorcycles and the modern materials and design genius of the same corps of German engineers which had designed the versatile and reliable all terrain mini-tanks. Their value had been proven against the murderous combination of elements which had all but conspired to thwart their efforts to stop the Soviet commandeered train and its cargo of Chinese missiles, eventually resulting in the derailment of the train, the loss of the stolen pre-War Chinese missiles and the death of Ivan Krakovski, then Karamatsov's effective second-in-command. Capable of cranking up to 160 mph on level, dry terrain, they were, like the mini-tanks, capable as well of maneuvering over the most rugged terrain, taking whatever nature might offer as a challenge, deep snow, loose mud, sand. He had requested that they be readied and they were.

Built to run on synth fuel and more fuel efficient than any motorcycle, regardless of power rating, had ever been in the past, a Special would virtually go anywhere.

And, to get the rider there and back again, each Special featured a precisely contoured armored fairing to protect the lower body, a high-rising windshield over this, fitted with defogger coils.

Built into the fairing on either side were twelve-inch barreled machineguns, like submachineguns in their diminutive size, firing the German major caliber caseless service round. Firing mechanisms were concealed within the handlebars. There was capacity for gear storage behind and on both sides of the saddle and, to a lesser extent, built into the fairing. Implaced just aft of the rear storage compartments were weapons pods, launching high explosive mini-grenades from the left pod, smoke or gas grenades from the right pod.

The fifth Special was gunmetal gray.

Despite his and Paul's vehement protests, Annie had insisted that she be allowed to accompany them, that she could ride a motorcycle as well as any of them. The argument consumed two minutes or less as the aircraft shut down and unbuttoned and, as Rourke, Annie and Paul exited the V-stol, he noticed that the machines had been joined by four figures, three of them unmistakably women, the fourth in traditional Chinese male attire with a heavy parka

170

over it.

John Rourke started walking across the runway, the wind blowing hard and cold, Chinese soldiers of the First City already beginning to unload the gear as he glanced back, noticing them for the first time, his attention focused elsewhere. One of the women was his wife, Sarah, and standing beside her, Natalia and, beside Natalia, Maria Leuden. The man was the Chairman of the First Chinese City.

Rourke reached the four who stood beside the five Specials and took Sarah into his arms, embracing her, kissing her hard on the mouth. "What's happened to Michael?"

"Annie felt—felt him getting injured. That's all I know. But it's enough." And he looked to Natalia Anastasia Tiemerovna. "Natalia—should you be—"

"My doctor says that healthy diversion is just the thing. Bjorn Rolvaag sends his compliments, by the way. He's recovering splendidly and more rapidly than anyone would have thought possible. I tried arguing them into bringing his dog up to see him, but no luck. Perhaps you could ask the Chairman."

John Rourke embraced her, kissing her lightly on the cheek, then took Maria Leuden into his arms. "He'll be fine, Maria. I know he will." She sniffed back a tear, smiled, kissed the cheek. He addressed the Chairman. "Sir, I am honored that you would come to meet us here. Who are the other two cycles for?"

Sarah Rourke cleared her throat. "I know I can't go. I was never that much for motorcycles anyway."

"I'm going, and Maria it turns out rode motorcycles in New Germany."

"Uh-huh," Rourke nodded. "The last place I want either of you is—"

"I'm going, John, with you or without you. And Maria—well—she can decide."

"If Michael's in danger, then I'm going so I can help get him out of it."

"Good for you, Maria," he heard his daughter saying as she hugged her mother, Paul leaning over and kissing Sarah Rourke on the cheek.

John Rourke looked at Annie Rourke Rubenstein. "We're going we don't quite know where against we don't quite know whom. It's not the ideal circumstances for a learning experience, hmm?"

"I'm going," Maria Leuden said, and Natalia started to laugh . . .

John Rourke stood beside the jet black Special, buckling on his gear. With the death of his Python, until he could get it restored, there had been only one logical choice in substitute armament. The hydrostatic shock value of the .357 Magnum fired from a six-inch barrel was something he relied on, despite his preference for his little Detonics .45s and his strong liking for the twin Scoremasters. But his only other Python was factory standard and he liked a revolver to be action-tuned for buttery smooth even double action and he liked a big bore revolver Magna-Ported. He could work the spare Python's action, with time, to the sort of trigger that he liked, but time was a luxury he could not afford now.

He elected instead to utilize one of the .44 Magnum revolvers, greater hydrostatic shock value and, if one knew how, nearly as controllable. John Rourke knew how.

The gun was a six-inch Smith & Wesson Model 629, not unlike the four-incher Michael carried. But, like his Python, it was action-tuned before the Night of The War by Metalife Industries and then the barrel slotted via the Mag-na-Port process for reduced perception of felt recoil and reduced muzzle climb. Fitted with the large size Pachmayr rubber grips, it felt essentially the same as the Python in the hand. Among the ammunition he had gotten the Germans to custom fabricate for him had been a considerable amount of the 180-grain jacketed hollow point duplicated after the Federal cartridge loading from five centuries before. His original intent had been that it would be for Michael's use. But now, that had changed.

He had taken Safariland speedloaders from the accessories cache, the ones Michael hadn't taken already, using four principally, carrying the rest of his spare ammo for the weapon boxed in MTM fifty cases.

The belt he'd selected was a single billeted one with a wide, double sided solid brass buckle, the holster one he had painstakingly preserved from the days before the Night of The War, hand-made, one of a kind, by Milt Sparks Leather. It was made entirely to his specifications to afford maximum protection in the field, the black full-flapped leather envelope riding the gun low in the leather, the flap completely protecting it like no commercially available holster could have done.

He buckled the belt at his waist over the arctic

parka now, the Crain LS X transferred from his trouser belt to the gunbelt for easier accessibility.

John Rourke straddled the machine, Sarah standing beside him. He kissed her hard. "I'll bring him back, Sarah."

"I know you will. I love you very much," and she threw her arms around his neck and Rourke held her tightly, her abdomen with the life it carried pressed close against him. "I know you will, but you come back, too, John."

"You've got a deal," John Rourke whispered, kissing his wife and holding her tight a moment longer. "And I love you." He looked to Paul and Annie, Annie's holsters buckled over her coat, Paul with the Schmiesser and an M-16 slung cross body on either side. Natalia, her double L-Frame Smith rig buckled over her coat, Maria Leuden with a Beretta 92F and an M-16. "God help us," he almost verbalized. He pulled on his helmet, the helmet's systems powered by electro-chemical energy from the body. He looked at the three women, Annie and Maria for a moment seeming ridiculous with their hair well below the levels of the helmets they wore, Natalia's hair shorter and stuffed up inside, he supposed. The microphone in the chin visor. He spoke into it. The system was multi-band, enabling two speakers to be heard at once. "Everyone on?"

The affirmatives came back through the interior of the helmet itself. He pulled down the visor and the tinted over-visor, his tinted darker than the rest, the automatic defogging systems taking over instantly, clearing them.

Sarah stepped back as he pulled on his gloves, then

174

twisted his right fist and revved the engine. John Rourke started the jet black Special ahead, the kick stand automatically releasing, uneasy over having Natalia so fresh from the hospital accompanying them, uneasy over Maria Leuden's inexperience, uneasy over Annie's safety and Sarah being left totally alone here, except for the injured Bjorn Rolvaag.

And uneasy over Michael. The ground was dry and flat.

John Rourke spoke into his helmet set. "Let's get these out to sixty nice and slowly. Natalia—keep an eye on Maria. Maria, sing out if you have trouble, any at all. Annie? Doing all right?"

"Fine, daddy."

"Take it easy—these are a lot faster than the Harleys, okay?"

"Okay—thank you for letting me come along."

"For letting you?" Rourke laughed, guided the machine off the surface of the field and glancing at the instrument package compass as he turned the fork to veer slightly right. "You're welcome—just do as you're told, kid," and he started building speed, the others on either side of him. "Paul—running okay?"

"I still like a Harley better."

Rourke laughed again, but it was forced.

The suppressed dual exhausts hummed as they moved in a pack over the cold-hardened ground, Rourke speaking into the headset again. "They'll do a hundred and sixty. We won't, but we need to get them to a little over a hundred and familiarize ourselves with the handling. Check your instrument package digital chronometers. Every sixty seconds, increase speed by five miles per hour until you reach

175

a hundred and five or unless you're experiencing difficulties. Acknowledge."

There were various words of understanding and agreement. "Begin—" he looked at the digital readout, "—now." Sixty-five, seventy, seventy-five, eighty, eighty-five. "Doing all right, Maria?"

"Yes, Doctor Rourke. I am doing fine, as you say."

"Good. Annie?"

"This is neat!"

"Concentrate on your driving."

Ninety, ninety-five, one hundred, one hundred-five. He held there, the ground starting to rise slowly now. "Any problems, excess vibration?"

No one expressed difficulty.

"Let's try the same method taking it up to one twenty-five and no further. The only three of us experienced enough, even with these machines, to take a bike higher are Natalia, Paul and myself. And no Mongol Pryzwalski horses are going to get anywhere near us. Go for one-ten."

One hundred ten, one hundred fifteen, one hundred twenty. One hundred twenty-five. "All right— still no problems—talk to me." There were no reported problems. The ground was levelling off here and they were already well away from the airfield. "On my signal begin a slow turn left, bringing speed down to ninety, then on my command open fire with your fairing guns, just a short burst from each to get the feel of them. Be ready. Start to decelerate. Start the turn." Rourke started banking the Special left, the brakes responding smoothly, evenly, the suspension so perfectly balanced that he could barely feel the motion. "Activate the safety now!" Rourke's right and left hand activated the twin machineguns simultaneously, the rocks at the far end of the plateau shattering under the impacts of the German caseless rounds, the sound of the gunfire compensated for by the helmet. "Cease fire!" Rourke ordered.

"John—no problems at all," Natalia told him.

"Good—keep an eye on Maria."

"She's doing fine, John."

"You feeling okay—you're sure?"

"Yes—I'm feeling wonderful. It's good to be doing something again," her voice came back.

Rourke said to all, "We're going to cut back right and keep a single file as we head toward the Second City. We're taking the route Michael, Han, Otto and the enlisted personnel took and we should cover their route in just a matter of hours because we'll be travelling so much faster than they were. Be your own best judge on speed, but especially you, Maria, don't push beyond your capabilities. We can cut speed without delaying ourselves very much."

"I understand, Doctor Rourke. Thank you. What speed should I try?"

"Let's keep it at one-o-five as long as it stays flat and even." They were into formation now, Rourke at the lead, peeling off, dropping his speed so the others would pass him and he could have a personal look at how Maria Leuden was handling her machine. As she passed him, he nodded to himself with approval, then increased speed to one hundred ten so he could overtake them all and resume the lead, swinging in, cutting back on speed again.

He looked at the instrument package digital. In a

few hours, they would know. If it had just been Paul, Natalia and himself, he would have risked closer to one hundred thirty, at least here. He shook his head, saying under his breath so the microphone wouldn't pick it up distinctly enough to be heard, "Patience."

His fists balled on the handlebars of the jet black Special he rode.

CHAPTER TWENTY-SIX

When he awoke, he realized his ankles were no longer shackled. When he tried to move, he realized his head had been bandaged and that he was reclining on a very soft bed or large couch.

"You saved my life, Rourke."

It was Prokopiev's voice, from behind him and Michael Rourke sat up, the pain a dull roar behind his eyes but manageable for now. He looked for Prokopiev. The Russian officer, in his BDU pants but with a white shirt draped over his shoulders, his right arm in a professional looking sling, his left arm outstretched beside him, sat on a stack of silk pillows by the far wall.

Michael swung his feet over the side. His boots and socks were by the edge of the bed.

"But more importantly," Prokopiev began again, "thank you for attempting to save the life of Corporal Kamerovski."

"The man with the chest wound—they—"

"Slaughtered him, yes."

"What about the man they had on the rack?"

"That was Senior Sergeant Yaroslav, an old friend as well as a valiant soldier and loyal Communist. They slit his throat as they carried us from the cell. I feigned unconsciousness because, then, I was unable to move. They treated my shoulder wound, cleaned it and bandaged it. I can use my left arm a little. She ordered them to care of us. Your head wound was cleaned and properly bandaged. You are fortunate to still be alive."

"Maybe. Who the hell is she?" Michael Rourke brought his feet to the level of the bed rather than attempting to lean over to get his combat boots on.

"I do not know. But she told me that I should relay this message. We will be publicly executed at dawn. I elected not to sleep. Rather enjoy my last hours alive while I'm awake."

Michael noticed that his watch had been returned, none the worse for wear. "Dawn, hmm? Well—lucky for us it's winter time. Maybe it'll be overcast." He cleared his throat. "I'm sorry about your friend. The sergeant. There wasn't anything—"

"You have placed me in a peculiar position. I am almost pleased we are dying. Otherwise, I would be faced with a severe conflict between duty and conscience. You are a brave man and I am forever in your debt."

"Forever doesn't promise to be too long. Any idea where our guns are?"

"No."

"Any idea why she cleaned us up instead of torturing us?"

"No. Perhaps she'll tell us. But you know how they do it. I refer, of course, to the method by which they execute."

Michael Rourke thought for a moment. "The classic Chinese methods of execution range from the headsman's axe to being thrown into a pit to be ripped apart by dogs. But I take it she told you?"

"At dawn, as you know, before the assembled population of the Second City. Perhaps that is why we were cleaned up. For a better show. Their method is barbaric but effective. We will be placed on the ground, hands and ankles tied to ropes, each of the ropes tied to the saddle of one of the Mongols, then the Mongols ordered to ride."

"It's a form of drawing and quartering. The Egyptians practiced it millennia ago."

"You are more knowledgeable of history than I."

"It goes with being five centuries old. I had lot of time to read," Michael smiled, trying to make himself think. "At dawn. Well—we've got maybe four hours to get ourselves out of here."

"Perhaps your two friends will bring the army led by your father and rescue you."

"Perhaps your two men will bring the army led by Colonel Antonovitch and do the same for you, Vassily."

Vassily Prokopiev laughed aloud. "There is a word in one of the old languages—"

"French—the word is 'touche'. No army?"

"Reconnaissance only for an impending military action, suffice it to say. And you?"

"No army. You were going to be extracted—a couple of gunships?"

"Yes. But they could have scared off General Wing's army satisfactorily."

"That the old guy's name—Wing?"

"Yes—she told me that, also that General Wing would be there to watch us executed for our merciless ambush of his column."

Michael had both boots laced and, slowly, tried to stand up. It didn't work instantly. "Any electronic

181

surveillance in the room? What's the status on guards?"

"Nothing electronic that I can detect. And there are two guards at the doorway just outside. The windows are barred and overlook a precipice of considerable height. Even if we were able to get through the bars, somehow, we would never be able to climb down without the most sophisticated climbing equipment, and certainly not I."

"Rappel?"

"Beneath us is the interior of the Second City. If we were not shot and did make it down, we would be recaptured or shot as soon as we did."

"Then, it's the door," Michael said brightly.

"I won't be much good to you in a fight, Michael."

"That's okay. You'll agree, since we're going to be executed and they've chosen a particularly nasty way to die, we have nothing to lose. Right?"

"Agreed."

"Right—give me a couple of minutes to get my head going." He slowly turned his head toward the doorway. It was an ordinary doorway, if slightly large and rather ornate. His father had always taught him that there was nothing to lose, in the face of certain death, by being as daring as circumstances would allow. He intended to test the theory.

He stood up, feeling slightly dizzy, his eyes scanning over the room for something that might be used as a weapon. There were pillows, there was a second bed, there was a long, slender tapestry that he imagined was some sort of bell rope—to summon the last hearty meal for the condemned. "Does she execute people often? I mean, is this death row we're in, you think?"

"Death row?"

"A place to wait until it is time for a death sentence to be carried out."

"I do not know."

"Don't have a knife or anything they didn't find, do you?"

"None whatsoever."

"Did she say we could call for a meal?"

"Yes. I'm not hungry—the medication, I think."

"I'm hungry. Probably throw it up, but I am hungry. It'd be too much to hope for that we could throttle a guard when the food was brought in, but maybe something with the food. I don't know. Anyway, if we're to be the entertainment at dawn, may as well make them work for it a little." He decided, as he walked slowly, slightly unsteadily across the room to pull the bell rope, that the next time he was under sentence of death, it would be decidedly better to have it occur in a country which traditionally used steak knives rather than chopsticks.

He tugged on the bell rope. After a second, the door opened and one Chinese regular shouted something unintelligible—unless one spoke Chinese—into the room. "Hungry—right?" And Michael Rourke rubbed his belly and made chewing motions with his mouth. The soldier grunted something that presumably meant he understood and closed the door. "Any line on the missiles?"

Prokopiev didn't answer for a moment, then, "Look out the window. Go take a look."

Michael Rourke walked toward the window, looked out and down, the bars well-set, the drop as steep as

Prokopiev had indicated, the city commons below. And far across the center of the Second City, he saw what first seemed like a smokestack surrounded by a church altar.

But it was an intercontinental ballistic missile and, although from the distance it was hard to tell for sure and he had seen such missiles in photographs, he thought there were people praying before it.

Michael Rourke closed his eyes.

CHAPTER TWENTY-SEVEN

Akiro Kurinami stood as Commander Christopher Dodd entered the room, Dodd's eyes meeting his, Wolfgang Mann's voice breaking the ensuing silence. "Sit down, Commander."

"Colonel Mann," Dodd began, not sitting down, not shifting his eyes from Kurinami's, "how dare you hold this man and his female accomplice in total defiance of my request!" His vituperation apparently spent, at least for the moment, Commander Dodd took a seat opposite Colonel Mann's borrowed desk in his borrowed office. His fingers drummed nervously on the chair arms. Kurinami retook his seat, at the far corner of the room, near the door. "I demand an explanation, Colonel," Dodd said, more evenly, more calmly.

"Lieutenant Kurinami? Would you care to provide an explanation?"

"Yes, sir," Kurinami said, standing again, his hand behind him as though at parade rest. "Doctor Halversen and I are the objects of a murder plot because I wisely duplicated the now blanked files in the Eden Project main computer. Without those duplicate records, only the persons responsible for blanking the files would know the locations of the strategic supply caches located throughout the United States, strategic fuel reserves and the like. I discovered the theft of a quantity of M-16 rifles, ammunition, food stores and medical supplies and other equipment. Because of all of this, I was kidnapped, forcibly detained and the attempt was made to have me divulge the location of the duplicate computer records. When this failed, Doctor Elaine Halversen, my fiance, was kidnapped, apparently to force my cooperation. I was able to free her, took her here for refuge. Then, before all the facts were known, I was to be turned over to Commander Dodd, along with Doctor Halversen. We fled, fearing for our lives, reached the Retreat of Doctor John Rourke. There, eight men, German nationals—"

"This is—"

"Preposterous? Let me finish, Commander, I implore you."

Dodd shook his head, but remained silent.

Kurinami continued. "Eight men, German nationals, fugitives from the legitimate government of New Germany, followed us, attempted to use explosives to gain entrance to the Retreat and were only foiled by the singular heroism of Doctor John Rourke, Doctor Rourke's daughter, Annie, and her husband Paul Rubenstein who caused the deaths of these eight men. They were utilizing M-16 rifles, most probably from among those missing from Eden Base inventory, German pistols and stolen German rocket launchers. These fugitive men included at least one man, Hans Weil, who is a known Nazi sympathizer and working for the violent overthrow of the government of New Germany.

"At Doctor Rourke's request," Kurinami went on, "Doctor Halversen and myself have been offered temporary political asylum by Colonel Mann acting on

186

behalf of Deiter Bern, president of New Germany."
Kurinami said nothing more.

"Is this true?"

"I was about to ask you much the same question,
Herr Commander Dodd," Mann smiled, lighting a
cigarette.

"The political asylum question!"

"Our base, because we are allies, is considered by
ourselves, at least, as a diplomatic legation, hence a
piece of New Germany here in your own land. We
feel well within our legal rights to offer endangered
persons political asylum, Commander." Mann offered
his cigarette case. "Forgive my rudeness, but I am
quite tired. Would you care for a cigarette?"

Dodd didn't answer. "What law do you refer to,
Colonel? There is no international law. Kurinami is
subject to the military discipline of Eden Base Command. He is mine. And so is his accomplice, Doctor
Halversen."

"Your use of the word, 'accomplice' fascinates me,
Herr Commander Dodd. It would appear that none
of the Eden personnel are unaccounted for, yet you
insist that the lieutenant has murdered someone.
Who might these dead be? German nationals who
are enemies of the state, wanted criminals, whom
you have chosen to give political asylum? Or, perhaps, with whom you sympathize?"

"I don't have to take your insults, Colonel."

"Indeed, you do not. Nor do I have to return
Lieutenant Kurinami and his fiance, the Fraulein
Doctor. Would you care for coffee? I can have it sent
around."

Commander Dodd stood, running his hands back

through his close cropped gray hair. "This tears it, Colonel. I want your base out of here, off American territory. Immediately."

Kurinami watched Colonel Mann's eyes. They remained impassive, the smile on his face unchanged.

"I will speak candidly also, if I may, Commander. If, for one moment, I thought you represented the just wishes of the Eden Base personnel, I would never have encouraged my government to set up this support facility in the first place. My opinion has not changed. If the people of Eden Base are polled— fairly—and my government is requested to evacuate this base, I can say without reservation that such will be done. If the good Herr Doctor Rourke were to tell us that we should leave, we assuredly would. I have no interest in your opinion, and less interest in your concerns. But I am very much interested in your affiliations with men such as the late Hans Weil. And, it is only out of respect for the survivors at Eden Base, and out of the greatest respect for Doctor Rourke, that I do not now have you arrested. Are you certain about the coffee, Commander?"

Dodd's body trembled with what was, unquestionably, rage. "You refuse to honor my request for the return of my prisoners, you refuse to honor my ultimatum for the removal of your base. You have not heard the last from me."

"Would that such were the case, Commander Dodd, I would truly rejoice. I take it you have pressing business elsewhere?"

Dodd wheeled on his heel, stared at Kurinami. "You little rotten son of a bitch. You can hide here, but you have to come out sometime. And then your ass is mine."

"I would gladly, Commander Dodd, with all due respect, accept your personal challenge at any time. Sir!"

"Get fucked," and Dodd stomped across the room, threw open the door and walked out.

Wolfgang Mann whistled softly, Kurinami staring after Dodd still. "That man is more than insane; he is dangerous."

It was stating the obvious, Akiro Kurinami almost said.

CHAPTER TWENTY-EIGHT

They rode on through the night, the vision intensification equipment within their helmets making the ground before them as bright as a cloudy day, but running lights of any kind unnecessary.

As they appeared a progressively narrowing gap, still several hundred yards away (they had reduced speed to fifty miles per hour as they had begun to climb), John Rourke spoke into the headset within his helmet chin guard. "Where the rocks narrow up ahead. It's a good spot for an ambush. Paul—you stay with Annie and Maria to back us up. Natalia—come up to the entrance to the gap with me, then wait until I'm through; cover me. Once I'm through, I'll radio back and cover you, then Paul, you bring Annie and Maria through. Any questions?"

"I can go through," Paul volunteered.

"I know you can—but it's my turn," and Rourke said nothing more, gradually accelerating to a little over sixty as Natalia pulled up alongside him, the others falling off as he looked back once. They slowed as the grade steepened, stopping their Specials at the entrance to the gap. "How are you feeling?" Rourke asked Natalia. Any and all could hear whatever words were exchanged between them over the commonly shared bands. "Tired?"

"A little. But I like these machines. It would be wonderful sometime, just to get on one and ride and ride and never stop until you reached a place where it was always green and people didn't want to kill one another, wouldn't it, John?"

"Maybe we'll all find such a place, someday. At least we can keep looking. You'll be all right out here?"

"Anything goes bad, I'll be right there with you," she told him and he turned his head to look at her.

But the helmet and visor were anonymous looking and he could see nothing of her face, nothing of her eyes, her hair. "I've always known that," John Rourke told Natalia Tiemerovna. He gunned the Special into the gap, reaching the high ground where it levelled and slowing to under twenty, his eyes scanning the ground. If tragedy had befallen Michael, this was as likely a place as any and more likely than most.

He brought the Special up short and stopped, skidding a little. "If you heard the skid, I'm fine," he said into his helmet radio. He dismounted as he kicked out the stand, keeping his helmet visors in place so he could see with the aid of vision intensification rather than the naked eye.

There was brass on the ground, both 5.56mm as was fired in the M-16s like Michael carried and 7.62X39, as was used with AK type weapons. Michael had indicated, after his accidental encounter with the Mongols, that they were armed with weapons of this type, but apparently of fresh manufacture, these and originals and copies of the Glock 17 9mm pistols. There were 9mm casings on the ground as well, but without detailed analysis he was unable to tell if they were from one of the Glock-types or from the Berettas carried by Michael.

191

The Metalife/Mag-na-Ported six-inch 629 in his right fist, he walked ahead, saying into his helmet radio, "I'm on foot. There are signs of a significant number of metallic cartridges having been fired here recently — the brass is untarnished. I'm going up the gap toward where it begins to narrow. First sound of a shot, it'll be a loud one from my revolver. But at the first sign, Paul, you get Annie and Maria up to high ground where they can cover. Natalia. You wait for Paul. Come in after me if I call."

There was a large, dark shape looming ahead on the ground. As he neared it, its shape was better defined. It was a dead horse, the carcass untouched, but the horse was too big for the horses that Michael and the rest of his party had utilized. It looked almost part Arabian. There was another dead horse about a hundred yards further along.

He looked toward the east and west elevations of the gap. Ambushers would logically have fired down from both sides. But where to take cover from which to return fire if the first rounds hadn't ended it, which apparently was the case? His eyes moved from side to side along the floor of the gap and, at last, he spotted a likely location, a sharply jutting overhang which would have protected anyone beneath it from enemy fire from above and afforded cover from behind which fire could be returned to the far sides of the gap.

John Rourke quickened his pace, his gloved right fist balling on the 629.

He stopped just before the rocks, .223 brass in abundance here, in greater abundance on the other side as he crossed over the rocks and down. He holstered his revolver and drew the Crain knife from its sheath at his left side, scraping with it on a rock surface that had caught his eye. Blood, dried.

"Natalia. See if you can get your machine up into the eastern side of the gap. Paul. You and Annie and Maria move up a little. I'm going up to the west side. And everybody be careful," he said needlessly.

He began to climb, carefully checking his footing as he moved, finding a solid purchase, climbing on, at last reaching the western summit.

Here, he found several bodies, Chinese and, judging from the socks one of the otherwise denuded bodies wore, German. And, curiously, a body that could have been Russian, again the only thing to tell by being the socks. Boots, trousers, winter clothes, even underwear were gone, not to mention weapons. He found considerable quantities of 9mm and .223 brass here.

"Natalia—you in position yet?" Rourke said into his helmet radio.

"Yes—there is no rifle brass, nor handgun brass. But there are plenty of Russian bodies. I can tell from the stockings. Otherwise, all the clothing and weapons are gone. Some of these men had their throats slit, others—"

"One man here is partially beheaded. A couple of dead horses down at the base of the rocks that I can see from here. Get back down. I'd like to say we could bury them, but there isn't time."

"Daddy—"

"What, Annie?"

"Michael was here—in that dream I had—I saw a place like this. He was here. I think this is where—

193

where—"

"Where it happened," Rourke finished for her. But what?

The only chance was to go to the Second Chinese City. And he hadn't brought an army. There hadn't been time for that, either.

"Paul—get on that other radio and get to Hartman's man at the Second City. See if he can shake us loose a couple of gunships to get within fifteen minutes striking range of the Second City and wait there for us to call them in."

"Right, John."

As he started down, John Rourke kept talking to them. "It looks like there was a battle here of considerable proportions. A lot of bodies, all Chinese—our Chinese, I'd say—and Russian. No sign of Michael, Han or Otto. The AK brass I found makes it look like the Mongols were in on it. So I do't have any idea what went on here, but I've got a bad feeling we don't have too much time to find out."

"Daddy—"

"What, Annie?"

"Michael's alive—I can feel it, somehow. I think he's trying to reach me—I know that sounds crazy—"

"No it doesn't," Natalia interrupted.

"I agree with Natalia. We wouldn't have been here at all to find this if it hadn't been for your dream. Just keep me informed on what you feel, what you think is happening, baby."

"All right, Daddy."

Rourke reached the base of the rocks in considerably less time than it had taken for him to make the climb, from above detecting a vastly easier route

194

down. As quickly as he could, he made his way past the strewn about brass, past the dead horses, toward his Special. And he looked at the luminous black face of the Rolex on his left wrist. In a little while, it would be light, perhaps making the task of finding out what was happening a little easier. But somehow, the thought of the sun rising made him shiver.

CHAPTER TWENTY-NINE

Han Lu Chen moved through the sparse crowds of those who were up before the rest of the Second City. There were old Mongols, too old to fight as mercenaries, not old enough to make a living as beggars, carrying harp shaped frames made of plastic or old pieces of metal tubing, trinkets and baubles, even food hung from them, trying to peddle their wares to others like them, the real customers not yet on the streets, likely not yet awake.

He shifted the weight of the pistol belt which carried his Glock and his saber, hooking his thumbs in the belt as he stopped to admire a piece of cheap jewelry.

The word was everywhere on the streets that at dawn there would be the execution of two foreign devils, one of the victims a Russian, the other an American. Most of the conversation that he overheard which did not gleefully focus on the means of execution focused instead on what an American might be. This was the first time he had ever penetrated into the Second City beyond the outer perimeter that lay just inside the gates. Han cared little what befell the Russian, but the American had to be Michael Rourke. In casual conversation around Mongol campfires, the Mongols had joked concerning the religion here in the Second City, that they worshipped a silly post.

But as he entered the common square, Han Lu Chen stopped, stared, powerless to do otherwise. He had never seen one fully assembled, standing, only the crated parts that time aboard the train. But he had seen pictures of such things.

These people did not worship a post, as the Mongols had joked about. What he saw upthrusting from the center of their temple was a ballistic missile.

A vendor offered him oral sex with a young girl for only a few coins. Han told the man, "I do not want her."

"A boy, then—I have two boys—"

"No," and he shrugged past the old Mongol. The Second City had its missiles, and they were about to execute Michael Rourke. He would have glanced at his watch, but to do so would have aroused suspicion since few Mongols told time by any means other than a sundial or an hourglass. It was only within the last dozen years that the Mongols had been elevated to their present exalted status of mercenary soldiers, before that a violent subculture treated as racial inferiors and afforded not even the most rudimentary learning.

And it couldn't be long now until dawn would come . . .

Otto Hammerschmidt had nearly given up hope. But he saw the Chinese Intelligence agent coming now, climbing up into the rocks, looking warily over his shoulder every few steps. Hammerschmidt wanted to shout to him, but a shout or any loud noise was well within earshot of any guards at the outer gates into the mountain and to betray his position would mean his own death and Han's as well. Any chance to locate Michael Rourke would die with them.

Hammerschmidt lit a cigarette, careful to shield the flame in the pre-dawn darkness, inhaling the smoke deep into his lungs. Where were the Russians? Even they were better than these, these savages.

Or, perhaps, the Soviet commander's men had not gotten through, perhaps been intercepted by more of the Second City military forces. There were two many things unresolved. Was Michael inside the Second City, dead or soon to be? Or was he somewhere in this vast rock wilderness, perhaps dead or dying by a mountain pass after the Mongols had tortured him?

Hammerschmidt admired Han Lu Chen's courage, to mingle among such devils as these. Hammerschmidt had seen the bodies left behind at the gap. It was not a battlefield, but a slaughterhouse, he thought.

He dragged heavily on the cigarette, Han almost out of sight of the entrance, almost up to him. He risked a loud whisper, "Well?"

Han didn't answer, clambered up over the high rocks in which Hammerschmidt had taken shelter, then dropped down into a crouch. "Michael Rourke is to be executed at dawn. He and a Russian officer will be taken out there into the open field before the main gates," and he gestured expansively toward the mud and rocks which dominated the landscape before the high gated main entrance into the mountainside, "and their wrists and ankles will be tied to Mongol saddles and General Wing, who commanded the army which captured them and killed all the others, will give the order for the Mongols to ride to the four winds. And Michael and the Russian officer will be torn limb from limb. A man can live for a short time after that, it is said, a very short time that would seem like an eternity. If nothing else, perhaps we could attempt to shoot them, mercy for them. But the distance is too far for the guns we have. And there is something else. They have the missiles, or at least one. They have it as an object of worship."

"An object—"

"Yes, Hammerschmidt. That is the cult started by the woman of the dragon robes. For years, it has been rumored that Mao himself no longer rules, but that a woman controls his every thought and that she had begun some strange religious cult. It is she who started using the Mongols as more than brigands. I—I—I do not know what to say. We—we must try, of course, must attempt to save their lives or kill them—but—but I cannot say how, Hammerschmidt." And Han Lu Chen bent his head into his hands.

Hammerschmidt, gently, then roughly, touched his hand to Han Lu Chen's shoulder.

CHAPTER THIRTY

The food was largely vegetarian, the meat so unidentifiable Michael Rourke elected not to touch any of the food. Vassily Prokopiev became nauseated merely looking at it. There were chopsticks for utensils. He knew now why they had returned his watch, so that he and Prokopiev could count the minutes remaining until their deaths.

And less than an hour's worth of minutes, at the outside, remained. And there was no way to tell how soon before that the guards would come for them.

When Prokopiev's vomiting subsided, Michael Rourke, able now to walk quite well, the pain in his head constant and unforgiving but manageable, squatted down in front of the chair into which Prokopiev had sunk. "Are you game to try?"

"There is nothing to lose. Yes. What is your plan, Michael?"

"Take that bucket you puked into, spill the contents onto the floor over by the window and lie down on the floor near it. I'll get them in here, somehow, and when they go to look at you, I jump them both. As soon as you hear it go down, try

200

and give me a hand. Okay?"

"But—"

"These chopsticks can make excellent thrusting implements. Centuries ago, there were men who could throw them and used them as weapons. I don't know how to do that, but to a weak part of the neck, to the solar plexus, the groin, into an eye or ear—they'll do some damage, maybe enough so we can get a gun or a blade. Then we play it by ear. Odds are good we'll get killed trying, but a death like that beats what they've got planned, right?"

"Yes. Should I lie down now?"

"Yes."

"Should we survive—"

"What?"

"I would regret someday killing you."

Michael Rourke clapped Prokopiev on the knee and smiled, "Well, you think you'd regret it!" He helped Prokopiev to his feet, then over toward the window, Prokopiev flexing his left fist in order to restore circulation.

They stopped beside the window, Michael looking down into the commons below. The missile was clearly in altar. Looking nearly as small as ants—he remembered the creatures from the time before the Great Conflagration—were women, performing some ritual before it.

He helped Prokopiev down, then went for the bucket which had been provided for their toilet use, which was now filled with vomit. Trying to close his nose—he felt nauseated himself—he spilled the contents across the floor near where Prokopiev lay. "Be ready, Vassily," Michael Rourke hissed.

The chopsticks, both sets, made of a type of plastic rather than wood, but rigid, were concealed up his sleeves. On impulse, he ran across the room and picked up a bowl of what could have been soup. It was still hot. He went back beside the door, looking for a place to put the bowl, at last setting it on the floor within reach, placing a cushion over it. There was no hard furniture of any kind. The food had been brought in by two regular army enlisted men, the bowls carried on trays, the trays taken away, the bowls set on the floor.

Michael Rourke began banging on the door. "Hey—he's sick, maybe dying—get him the hell out of here! He's throwing up all over everything! Come on, damnit!" If one of their number spoke English, however stiffly, like the woman with the dead eyes, then it was always possible someone outside the door spoke English as well. "Come on! It smells in here! Open up!"

The door began to open, the two unpleasant looking Mongols he had seen earlier stepping partially into the room. One of the men began to crinkle his nose at the smell of the vomit.

"See what I mean? This smells like shit—worse than that! Maybe I'm gonna be ripped limb from limb, but I shouldn't have to put up with this. Come, on—"

The other guard—apparently the smell bothered him less—gestured for Michael to step back, grunting something Michael didn't understand. Michael stepped closer to the hidden bowl of soup. The guard passed him, the second man coming closer.

Each was armed with a pistol and a saber, both men with their pistols drawn. As the second guard came even closer, Michael let one of the chopstick pairs slide out of his cuff, the other pair more secure under the band of his Rolex.

Michael turned to face the guard, saying, "The poor guy's dying, but what a smell—" Michael's right hand arced upward and both chopsticks in his right hand rammed into the Mongol's left eyeball, the Mongol's gun discharging as Michael threw himself to the floor, flipping the pillow away, the first guard wheeling around toward him, Michael hurtling the bowl of hot soup—it wasn't scalding—into the first guard's face. As the first guard's mouth opened to scream or curse, his pistol discharged, but Michael was already moving, the second pair of chopsticks in his hand. He threw himself against the first guard, fluid from the eyeball dribbling down the man's cheek, the chopsticks that had been rammed into the eye gone. Michael stabbed the second set of chopsticks into the first man's throat, both hands, one holding the pistol, automatically moving to protect the face. Michael's right knee smashed upward and his hands grabbed for the saber, tearing it from the leather scabbard, wheeling toward the first guard, throwing the saber like a javelin, the saber impaling the first Mongol through the chest. Michael's body slammed into the second man, knee smashing him again as they fell to the floor.

There was another shot, but there was no time to wonder about it. Michael's hands closed over the Mongol's gunhand and his right elbow snapped into the adam's apple, the fingers of his left hand closing over the little finger of the Mongol's right hand, snapping it back, breaking it, the gun falling away.

With the heel of his right hand, Michael punched upward against the base of the Mongol's nose, breaking the bone, driving it upward into the brain. His left hand closed on the butt of the Glock 9mm and he rolled.

Vassily Prokopiev was kicking the first guard in the face repeatedly.

The eyes were already wide open and the saber was still thrust through the Mongol's chest. "We've gotta get outa here. Grab his extra ammo. Hurry." Michael was to his knees, quickly searching the dead Mongol beside him. The eye still oozed fluid and Michael felt more nauseated than he had before.

He found two spare magazines for the pistol. He ran across the room, helping Prokopiev with getting the magazines. "Just pull the trigger. Totally passive safety system," Michael Rourke advised.

The corridor outside would be filled with guards in under fifteen seconds, he guessed. His left hand closed over the saber and wrenched it from the Mongol's chest. "Take the one at his belt. Hurry."

"You go ahead—I—"

"Nuts," Michael declared, running for the door, the Glock 17 in one hand, the saber in the other. He could hear sounds of running feet, but saw no one yet, the corridor bending less than ten yards away. There could have been an army around the bend. Vassily Prokopiev was beside him. Michael stepped into the corridor. "That way," and he nodded toward the opposite end of the corridor from which he heard the sounds of running feet, Prokopiev beside him, moving too slowly. But Michael Rourke had no intention of leaving the man behind, KGB officer or not. Human beings, he had been raised to believe, didn't do that sort of thing to other human beings, regardless of who they were.

They reached the end of the corridor, the sounds behind them louder now. There, where the corridor abruptly stopped, was a stairwell, the stairs leading interminably downward it seemed, corridors branching off from the ever circling stairs periodically. But at the center of the stairwell, reachable by walking out on a wheel-spoked shaped platform, was a firepole.

"Time to play Batman?"

"Batwhat?"

Michael looked back down the corridor, coming around the bend a small army of Mongols, rifles and sabers brandished, animal-like noises coming from their lips.

"Tell you about the Caped Crusader later, okay. Shove the gun in your pants and give me a thirty second start, then do what I do."

"All right—"

With the saber's edge, Michael cut away the bandages beneath the sling which braced Prokopiev's dislocation, keeping the right arm bound to the right side at the upper arm, the forearm slung. "Hold onto the sling for later. But you'll need both hands now. This won't feel good." And he moved Prokopiev's arm outward.

Prokopiev sucked in his breath like a scream and

his knees buckled, but with Michael's help he remained standing.

"Get out there — and give me your saber."

Prokopiev started out along one of the spokes of the wheel, the spoke ending at a large central ring, within which the pole was set. "You have to hold on just tight enough to slow your rate of descent, or otherwise you'll hit bottom like a stone."

"You have done this before?"

"Nope — but I watched a lot of television in the last five hundred years." The Mongols were coming. Michael took up his saber and hurtled it down the corridor, the saber fended off by one of the Mongol rifles. "Be ready! Thirty seconds — remember!" He threw the second saber, the blade slicing across the right arm of one of them, the man falling back. Michael fired the Glock 17, a half-dozen rounds sprayed down the corridor, the Mongols falling back for an instant. Stuffing the Glock into the side pocket of his BDU pants, he flipped the railing and entered the wheel, stepped over the central rail and held to the pole. He looked upward, the staircase spiraling several stories higher, the pole jutting to the top floor as well. The Second City had, he presumed, been built into a mountain upward, similar to the German enclave in Argentina, and was of totally different design than the First Chinese City. "Give them a half-dozen shots, watch how I do it and go for it. Good luck."

"And to you, Michael Rourke."

Michael grabbed the pole more tightly and jumped, the pole's composition of some sort of plastic, not unlike that used in the chopsticks he

206

had improvised as weapons. His hands felt no heat from friction, his knees and ankles locked around it easily, the sensation of a controlled fall not totally unpleasant. He looked up, hearing shots, seeing Prokopiev take to the pole.

Michael looked below him, and suddenly there was a Mongol face and a saber pointing upward at him. Clutching tighter to the pole with his left hand, his chest pressed against it, Michael's right hand went to the side pocket of his BDU pants for the gun, the snag-free design of the Glock 9mm paying off as he tore it free. He fired, then again and again, the saber point mere feet below him now as he sped downward toward it, then the saber falling away and the Mongol tumbling after it, down along the length of the pole toward the bottom still more than a hundred feet below. He tried stuffing the pistol away, but couldn't, taking his finger out of the trigger guard, clutching the gunhand to the pole as well, skidding, sliding, heat finally starting to build up on his flesh. He was going too fast.

Below him, the Mongol's body impacted the floor surface, bounced, then jammed half inside the wheel at the base of the pole.

Michael tried slowing himself, but when he had clung to the pole with only one hand, he had gathered too much momentum. He couldn't slow himself.

The bottom was rushing up toward him as he clutched his booted feet to the pole, a scraping sound filling his ears, then impact, his feet crashing against the Mongol's shoulders, dislodging the body,

Michael sprawling to the ground, the wind knocked out of him.

He turned his head, his head aching more intensely, the dead Mongol staring back at him, the skull neatly cracked and blood trickling down across the forehead and the bridge of the nose. "Thanks for the help," Michael gasped, to his feet, coughing, doubling over.

Prokopiev—Michael swayed toward the base of the pole, pocketing his gun, Prokopiev coming too fast. There was nothing else for it, Michael reaching down, dragging the hulking dead man into the wheel at the base of the pole, then stepping back, Prokopiev impacting the dead body, bouncing away from it and sprawling across the floor in a skid.

Michael drew his pistol, ran to Prokopiev. "Go on! I am done!"

"Bullshit!" Michael Rourke reached for the wounded arm, hauling it across his shoulders, Vassily Prokopiev wincing with the pain as Michael hauled him to his feet.

"I can hold them off—run for your own life."

"Shut up!" Michael started ahead, Prokopiev's left wrist locked in Michael's left fist, Michael's right hand holding the partially shot out Glock 17. But there was no time to change magazines.

They were in what seemed to be some sort of lobby, beyond it a doorless entryway and beyond that the commons Michael had seen from above. A siren was beginning to sound, like one of the old air raid sirens he had heard as a child in the days before the Night of The War.

He was almost running, dragging Prokopiev who

could, it seemed, barely walk, Prokopiev's face dripping sweat despite the cool temperatures of the air here.

They were through the lobby, into the commons, old Mongol vendors everywhere, younger people, dressed alike in peasant clothes looking like pajamas, soldiers rushing through the rapidly dissipating crowd. Michael fired two shots into the air, screams panic. Panic would slow the progress of the soldiers, even if just a little.

They were midway along the commons, the white robed women he had seen from above as the size of ants now clearly discernible, braziers, smoke rising from them, placed before the base of the missile, the women running in panic as Michael dragged Prokopiev toward them, the shrine, if that was what it was, near the gates leading out of the commons— to what?

One of the women screamed. Michael pumped two more shots into the air, rammed the pistol into his beltless waistband. "Gimme your gun—can you reach it."

"My waistband—I am sorry, Michael."

Michael Rourke nearly dropped Prokopiev as he twisted his right hand for the gun, grasped it, ripped it free, fired twice behind him into the air over the heads of the oncoming soldiers but to avoid hitting bystanders.

The gates were less than a hundred yards off, but already starting to close. He quickened his pace. "Move those feet, soldier! Now!" Prokopiev was trying, lurching forward, Michael only half-dragging him now.

Fifty yards, the gates nearly shut. A Second City regular was dragging at one of the gates, to close it faster. Michael shot him with a double tap from the Glock, the Maoist's body tumbling sideways and into the path of the automatically closing gate section, blocking it, a loud pneumatic hum getting louder as the machine strained against the obstacle.

Michael looked behind him. He'd come back if he made it. The missiles. The strangely evil looking, beautiful looking woman — they had his guns, the knife old Jan had made for him. He'd be back.

To the gates, dragging Prokopiev through the gap, Michael letting Prokopiev fall to his knees for an instant, dragging the partially crushed body of the Maoist away from the gate, the gate slamming shut so rapidly Michael almost lost his left hand to it.

They were in the open now, a vast field, some sort of platform set up near the far right side — to the west, he thought. It was gray banded darkness just before the sun would wink over the horizon.

There were high rocks five hundred yards or so distant. He grabbed Prokopiev's wrist and hauled the man fully over his shoulder into a fireman's carry, Prokopiev sucking in his breath against the pain.

Michael threw himself into a heavy, shallow strided run, Prokopiev's stolen Glock in Michael's right fist.

He heard something like thunder. He didn't look back. The thunder grew louder. He pushed himself harder into the run, firing blindly behind him, running.

The thunder was nearly upon him. Michael Rourke looked back. Mongol horsemen, riding down hard on him, in their hands, stretched between them, a net. Michael fired, one of the ponies stumbled, regained its balance, the two riders out of sync now, Michael firing again, but wildly this time, running on.

"Michael!"

It was Prokopiev's voice. Michael Rourke looked back, the net hurtling over them, the horses closing on them, Michael's balance going as he fired out the Glock, Prokopiev slipping from his shoulder, falling, Michael stumbling, the net suffocatingly tight around him.

He tried reaching for the other Glock. There were a few shots left in it, but his right hand was bound up in the netting. A rifle butt arced downward toward his face—

CHAPTER THIRTY-ONE

Nicolai Antonovitch sat at his field desk. It was no more than a table.

The senior ranked among the pilots to have extracted Prokopiev and his reconnaissance party stood off to the side, the lieutenant, who along with a private soldier, had reached the rendezvous, standing at rigid attention immediately in front of the desk.

"When the squadron overflew the battle zone, if I understand you correctly, Comrade, there was nothing but carnage on either side of the gap. Correct?"

"That is correct, Comrade Colonel. In the far distance, as we climbed, a large party of men mounted on horseback could be seen, riding in the direction of the Second Chinese City."

"And you inspected the battle area?"

"That is correct, Comrade Colonel. The body of the young American, Rourke, was nowhere to be found, nor the bodies of the comrade major, nor of Senior Sergeant Yaroslav. Two private soldiers were missing as well."

"And you have no knowledge as to the whereabouts of the Chinese civilian and the German officer who went to locate this army the young Rourke spoke of?"

"That is correct, Comrade Colonel. No attempt was made to follow them, as I was under strict orders by the comrade major to make all haste to the rendezvous site. Afterward, no trace of them could be seen from the air, nor any trace of the army which the young American referred to."

"And," Antonovitch said, looking at the senior pilot, the squadron leader, "the clogged fuel line caused one of your craft to be forced down and, following standard procedures, all of your flight landed and waited while the fuel line was repaired, this necessitating a delay of some two hours."

The officer stepped forward. "Yes, Comrade Colonel. That is what happened."

"No one is at fault here, except perhaps Prokopiev for naively trusting a Rourke. And, it would appear, Prokopiev, Rourke and the other personnel are likely prisoners of Second City forces." He was thinking out loud, he knew, but Prokopiev's number two, Nikita Achinski, a captain, could lead the raid on the Second City.

"Nothing has changed," Antonovitch declared, rising, both men already at attention stiffening, raising their heads. "Rejoin your respective units. You — instruct Captain Achinski to join me here in five minutes." Antonovitch looked at his watch. "The attacks will begin on schedule. Carry on."

He had no choice, the commitment too great now . . .

* * *

They had watched it, powerless to intervene, Han forcibly restraining him. Hammerschmidt cursed the luck.

And now he waited as he watched the crowds assembling before the gates of the Second City, through his binoculars able to see Michael's face, bruised and bleeding, and the Russian held up beside him. A woman with long dark hair walked past them and then on toward the platform at the far edge, attended by a group of women in white robes and surrounded by a group of Mongols. Where was Han? Hammerschmidt lit a cigarette . . .

Han Lu Chen moved along the far edges of the crowd. He had originally hoped to throttle one of the Mongols privately, then steal clothing for Hammerschmidt, but it all moved too fast. There would be no time for any of that. The sun was rising and the four horses with their heavy, studded saddles, four of the Arabian mixes, powerful and fast, were already tethered at the four compass points. They were going to kill one first, then the other.

The woman with the dragon robes—it had to be her—rose to the platform, General Wing joining her, thousands of civilians and hundreds of troops, both regular army and Mongol mercenaries, mingling among the crowd, a solid phalanx of Mongols between the platform and the citizenry.

As he worked his way closer, he could see Michael and the Russian commander, Prokopiev, being brought forward, Michael under his own power,

214

Prokopiev virtually dragged, his legs unmoving.

Han Lu Chen's mind raced.

If he could reach the platform area and create a diversion—but was Michael strong enough to attempt another escape. And to where.

Han kept moving. If he could reach the platform, somehow get to the woman in the dragon robes or Mao when he arrived, put a gun to one of their heads. It was the only thing he could think of and he didn't think it would work.

Mao ascended the platform . . .

John Rourke consulted the map overlay on the instrument package. He spoke into his helmet radio. "We'll be in sight of the Second City in another few minutes. But we'll head up into the rocks near it shown by the German overflights. We can make plans for penetration when we arrive. Follow me," and he made the Special veer left, toward the rocks he could already see in the distance, cutting speed and actuating the muffler constriction to further reduce noise level.

It was charging into nowhere, but he had no choice. But, perhaps, observing the entrance to the Second City from the rocks nearby would tell him something.

"Daddy—Michael's in terrible pain. I can feel it."

"I know, sweetheart," he whispered back into his radio.

CHAPTER THIRTY-TWO

Mao spoke.

The woman with the dragon robes, surrounded by her white robed ladies, smiled serenely.

Michael Rourke stood solemnly, the Russian standing but only because he was supported on either side by one of the Mongols.

Han listened as he worked his way closer to the platform.

"These Russian mercenaries led a death squad from the First City. Under questioning by inquisitor Xaan-Chu—" Han assumed Xaan-Chu was the tall, evil looking man in black pajama-like uniform with a ceremonially decorated sword handing at his left hip who stood near to the woman with the dragon robes. Han had never seen Xaan-Chu, but knew that he was supervisor of security and interrogations. Even the Mongols he had infiltrated among spoke of Xaan-Chu in hushed tones of fear. "—they revealed their plans. A force from the First City is coming to attack us in our homes. For this reason, I declare that all men under the age of forty are to report for the taking up of arms, all women over the age of twenty who are childless are to do the

216

same. We shall meet the revisionist devils and destroy them before they can come to the Second City and rape our women and slaughter our children. And the heads of these two Russian mercenaries, once their bodies have been torn into the four winds, shall ride before us as a warning of the savage justice of the Second City dispensed to all those who would attack us. I offer these weapons found on the two who are about to die to the first among you who will step forward to destroy them." And as he spoke, he raised Michael's still holstered guns, his knife, even his musette bag into the air over his head, as he raised each item murmurs of admiration and comments on the good fortune of the riders who were to be the executioners coming spontaneously from among the spectators, civilian and military alike.

The weapons of the Russian officer got slightly less envious comment.

"Who will first mount stout horse and ride?"

Han Lu Chen was near to the phalanx of horse guard Mongols and he vaulted forward, jumping upward, shouting, "I will ride. My brother was killed by them! I will ride or kill the man who tries to stop me!"

A Mongol from the crowd twice Han's size half-drew his saber and shouted a cursed challenge, Han drawing his own blade. But Mao's voice thundered down from the platform. "The small one! Let him come forward!" There were cheers and boos and hisses and catcalls as the phalanx parted and Han flipped nimbly up onto the platform. And he stood before Mao, the old eyes dark, dancing with hatred and amusement. "Your name."

Han thought of one. "I am Kang, great Mao!"

"Kang—" He seemed to roll the name on his tongue. Mao raised his voice and addressed the multitude. "Kang will ride!" There was cheering now, shouts of encouragement. Mao looked at him sideways. "Take what you wish from among these trinkets, Kang."

Han Lu Chen bent over the low table on which they had been replaced after Mao had raised them to the covetous crowd. He took Michael's double shoulder holster with the Berettas, slinging it over his own shoulders. He took Michael's pistol belt with the four-inch .44 Magnum revolver and the survival knife. He cinched it to his left side, the revolver slung behind his saber hilt, the knife beside his holstered Glock automatic. He gathered up the loose spare magazines, the leather case of magazines, then the loaders for the revolvers, putting these in the stuff sack slung from his left shoulder. He took the musette bag, slinging it to his body.

His eyes caught Michael's eyes as he looked up to face Mao. "Great one. I leave these other fine weapons for the other riders." He could carry no more.

"Kang leaves these other weapons for the other riders. Two rifles and a handgun of stainless steel, a stout knife, much ammunition! Who steps forward to ride?"

There were more volunteers than the phalanx of guards could hold back, Han looking again at Michael while the volunteers were selected as Mao pointed to them.

Michael didn't even acknowledge. Had he been drugged? Was that why the Russian seemed so lifeless.

The three volunteers were selected. Han stood at their head, the woman with the dragon robes coming forward and standing in front of him, raising her hands to the multitude who became instantly quiet. "The Maidens of The Sun will escort these valiant riders to their steeds, and pray as the evil ones are ripped to the four winds!" There was a cheer from the crowd, and the women in the white robes who served the temple came forward and the prettiest among them—but her eyes were lifeless—took Han's hands in hers and led him across the platform, down the low steps, toward the horses. He chanced a look back. Michael Rourke was being taken forward . . .

John Rourke edged along the rocks, the man-shape hidden there closer now. With the dark clothing, in the poor light, he could not tell the uniform, simply assumed the worst and hoped that it was perhaps Hammerschmidt, or perhaps even his son, that somehow Annie—

He closed the gap, Natalia's suppressor-fitted Walther PPK/S .380 in his right fist. In Russian, then quickly in English, Rourke hissed, "Move and you are dead!"

The man-shape froze.

"Herr Doctor?"

Hammerschmidt. "Otto? Otto!" Rourke moved quickly toward him, dropping down to cover, thousands of people gathered before the gates of the Second City in front of a large platform. "Where's Michael?"

Hammerschmidt gave him the glasses in his hands. Rourke brought them to his eyes as Hammerschmidt simply said, "There, Herr Doctor."

CHAPTER THIRTY-THREE

The woman with the dead eyes and the fancy robes looked into his face, her curious English again as she spoke. "It is a pity the execution needed to be public, because the pit would have been a good challenge for someone like you. Perhaps the best fight we have seen."

"The pit?"

"Hungry dogs. You can fight them before they kill you."

"Gee—well, maybe next time," Michael told her, forcing a smile he didn't feel.

"You are first. I will lead you there. But, if you touch me, the eyes of your friend will be gouged from his face before he is killed."

"I wouldn't touch you. I might not be able to wash my hands," Michael responded.

She slapped his face. He stood there, saying nothing, his hands bound behind him.

She started ahead and he fell in behind her, across the platform, down the steps, Mongols on all sides of him except ahead, two Mongols flanking the woman. Her hair swayed over her back as she walked.

221

He looked ahead, Han already mounted on a strapping gray mare, one of the white robed girls with the clouded eyes holding the reins of his horse. He wondered what Han had in mind. It was just as fatal to be ripped apart three ways as four, he thought soberly.

Michael Rourke kept walking.

They stopped between the four horses.

She turned to him. "You might choose to struggle against the ropes. It will please those who are watching."

"You bet."

His hands were unbound, but his wrists weren't released, simply rebound, one to one rope, one to another, each of the ropes leading to one of the mounted horses, the one from his right arm leading to Han's. He was forced down to his knees, then flat to the ground, a saber at his throat. But his arms could still move. His ankles were tethered now too, one rope leading to each of the other two horsemen and their animals.

Flat on his back, he looked up into the sky for a moment. "Are you sure the sun's really up? Doesn't look like it to me," he said to her, his mind racing. He could attempt to drag off the second rider with the rope leading from his wrist, but the ropes on his ankles? What could Han do?

"The sun is up. Good-bye, American." The woman smiled, her eyes a window to incarnate evil, he thought.

He looked at Han Lu Chen. Then white robed girls stepped away from the horsemen . . .

* * *

Maria Leuden had given up her motorcycle to Otto Hammerschmidt, not even time to adjust the helmet to fit him. Paul had dismounted the field radio from the back of his machine, instructing Maria how to call for the helicopter gunships he had requested be in waiting and to tell them to hurry.

Natalia had already moved up, beside John Rourke. She could not see his face with the helmet that he wore. His parka was off, left with Maria Leuden, his double shoulder holsters exposed over the heavy sweater, the sweater bunched up in front and the Detonics Scoremasters in the waistband of his trousers.

"Time is up—we move out," John Rourke announced, Natalia hearing his voice through the headset. Her heart was beating rapidly and she felt a lightheadedness. She supposed it was action after all— "Let's go!" And John Rourke's jet black Special rocketed ahead, Natalia throttling out, just slightly behind him, Paul and Annie on the left flank, Otto Hammerschmidt on her right.

It was a hastily conceived plan. As they entered the valley, coming down out of the rocks, they began to execute it, Paul and Annie breaking off toward the platform, Otto, Natalia falling in beside him, toward the far side of the open expanse, John Rourke going right up the middle, as he always did . . .

Michael Rourke's head screamed at him with pain. He didn't know what the signal would be, for

223

the execution to begin. Michael did nothing—he didn't want to ruin Han's plan, if there was one. He could wait no longer, the ropes tensioning slowly outward.

He tugged at the rope that led from his right wrist, the rope Han had, the rope sliding free, Michael shouting, "Han—a knife!"

Han Lu Chen's animal wheeled, Han riding down on him, Michael reaching for the rope from his left wrist, grabbing at it as the other three horses started to run.

The hammering of hooves, Han's saber flashing, a rope cut, Michael's left hand free now, but already he was being dragged, the rope on his right leg nearly taut as was the one from his left. He heard gunfire, automatic weapons, to his right a jet black motorcycle, coming right toward him.

Han's saber slashed again, the rope from Michael's left ankle cut, but now Michael was being dragged, hands and elbows locking around his head and face to protect it, his shirt ripping away from his body, rocks gouging at him. He could see Han, riding in the dust of the one remaining executioner, Han's pistol firing, the reins to his mount held in his teeth, the rider falling, the horse stumbling. Michael threw himself forward, grabbing at the rope with both hands, heaving it, the animal up, vaulting ahead now, Michael's arms nearly ripped from the sockets, the rope tensioned between his ankle and his hands, his body torn across the ground.

He saw Han, trying to gain on the animal, saw the jet black motorcycle, one of the Specials, the one his father rode, closing, cutting through mounting Mongol horsemen, Maoist soldiers kneeling to fire their rifles.

The horse dragging Michael Rourke ran wildly onward toward the rocks, the hum of the Special louder now, nearly alongside him as Michael struggled to raise his head, his grip going, his hands bleeding where the rope abraded them.

He thought he heard his father's voice, telling him, "I'm coming, son."

The jet black Special passed him, dust flying into his face, rock chips spitting up toward him, his father's left gloved hand moving, a flash of gleaming metal, a handgun, the handgun discharging, then again and again and again, the horse slowing, the handgun still firing, the horse spilling, head first, almost cartwheeling, Michael whipped right into the path of his father's motorcycle, the Special veering just past him, skidding, his father jumping from the saddle as it spun out. Michael rolled over onto his back, his head . . .

Natalia Tiemerovna wheeled her machine toward John Rourke, the Mongol riding up on him throwing away his astrakhan hat. It was Han. But from behind him, a dozen riders were bearing down toward John and Michael. Natalia worked the firing mechanism on both machineguns, their roar barely audible because of the protection afforded by the helmet, men and horses tumbling to the ground.

To her left, Otto Hammerschmidt was driving into a knot of footsoldiers, his machineguns blazing. To her right, what seemed like an endless stream of soldiers were pouring from the gates of the Second City.

She turned the motorcycle in an almost too fast arc, activating the high explosive grenades in the rear weapons pods, launching, explosions rippling over the ground before the entrance. She arced the machine again, activating the second pod, firing the mixed smoke and gas, holding her breath as she drove through the flames where bodies burned from the high explosives, her machineguns blazing toward more riders coming down on John and Michael.

She could see Annie and Paul, Paul's machine rocking across the steps leading onto the platform, guns blazing, white robed women there fleeing, Mongols dying. Annie was right behind him. They were going after the Russian officer, she realized.

She thought she caught sight of Paul getting the man onto Annie's machine, then remounting. But she had to turn her machine, cutting a wedge now between a platoon strength-sized group of uniformed soldiers and where John and Han helped Michael onto the back of John's Special.

She read the digital counter for rounds remaining, both machineguns nearly emptied now. She fired a second volley from the gas and smoke package, cutting a narrow arc, balancing out her machine with her feet as she turned it quickly, accelerating past them again, activating the second package in the high explosives pod, the mini-grenades plowing across the ground as they exploded in series on impact, making the dirt and rocks between her and the soldiers rise momentarily like a wave.

She turned her bike, her heart beating so rapidly in her chest that she could feel it pounding against her left breast, her mouth so dry she could not swallow, pain behind her eyes.

"I love you John," she said into her helmet radio. "I always will, love you, John. John! John!"

Her mind, she knew, was working on two levels, on one she was rationally aware of turning her Special right and firing into a pack of Mongols on foot, but on the other level—"John . . . I'm so lonely without you, John . . . John—hold me . . . Please hold me again. Ohh please."

"Natalia—what's the matter," his voice came back to her. His machine was moving again.

She could hear Maria Leuden's voice. "The chief of the helicopter pilots has radioed back, Doctor Rourke. He and the other two pilots encountered a massive Soviet force closing on the Second City. Two helicopters already shot down, his on fire and out of control. We have no help coming."

"Stay concealed in those rocks."

"Daddy—we've got the Russian officer. He's more dead than alive, I think."

"Head out of here."

"John—please love me." More of the Maoist foot soldiers, firing at her, bullets bouncing off her fairing. Natalia fired out her machineguns and the counters readout empty.

She stopped her machine, slinging her M-16 forward. "I don't—ohh, John, I hurt—" Her chest was tightening and her head ached beyond any pain she had ever known as she opened fire, the M-16 to her shoulder.

"Natalia — get outta there — we're clear. Get outta there!"

"John —" she kept firing, one of the M-16s empty. She let it drop on the sling to her side taking up the one on her left side, firing it from the hip.

Terror seized her and she was crying and the rifle fell from her hands and she fell from the saddle. "John!"

She was two people, the one who watched and the one who cried . . .

John Rourke was listening to Natalia losing her mind. "Natalia!" But she no longer answered him.

He slowed his Special, Otto Hammerschmidt to his far left, but no helmet radio through which Hammerschmidt could be contacted.

Rourke veered toward the German commando captain, pushing up the visors on his helmet, shouting now into the wind, "Hammerschmidt! Take Michael! Hammerschmidt! I'm going back for Natalia! Hammerschmidt! Hammerschmidt!" And Hammerschmidt's borrowed Special started to turn, Rourke's machine intersecting with it, Hammerschmidt stopping, Rourke's machine stopping. "Take Michael!"

"I can get her, Herr Doctor!"

"No — only me!" Rourke was out of the saddle, shifting Michael's unconscious form onto the back of Hammerschmidt's bike, giving Hammerschmidt half the length of rope by which he had tied Michael in place. "Get up into the rocks, start marshalling people together. Get Maria on a bike. Start heading

228

out. Cut a tangent to the east and you should avoid Soviet gunships. I'll catch up to you. Be on the lookout for Han. Hurry. Paul's in charge." Rourke didn't wait for a reply, jumping back aboard his machine, pulling down the visors. He sheathed his Crain knife and stuffed the rope down inside his sweater.

As he gunned the machine into a tight turn, Rourke rasped into his headset, "Take off out of here on a tangent from here in the direction of the First City but eastward. I'll catch up with you. Don't wait. I'm bringing Natalia."

"Daddy—what's wrong with her—"

"Never mind—Paul? Can you hear me?"

"Gotchya."

"You're running things until I catch up. Get everybody outta there quick and don't use the radio you left with Maria. They could triangulate in on us."

"Let me—"

"I'm doing this alone. Take care of Annie." Already, Rourke's machine was bearing down on Natalia's position, his guns still carrying over a half load.

Behind him, troops were pouring from inside the Second City. He decided to fix that, activated the high explosive weapons pod, blowing out the first package, the ground vibrating around him and, as he glanced back, smoke and flames belching skyward.

"John—I'm—John—John—John—"

Natalia's voice.

Rourke cut a swath between her position and the

229

advancing Maoist regulars, firing off the second high: explosive package, driving them back. Han was riding toward her on horseback.

Rourke arced back right, throwing up his visors. "Han! Take Natalia's machine! Han!"

The Chinese Intelligence agent waved back at him, his mount drawing up short as he dropped from the saddle, falling prone beside Natalia, grabbing up one of her M-16s and firing, drawing her back behind her machine, firing again, the M-16 empty now, Rourke looking back, the Maoist regulars advancing once more. Rourke fired one of the gas/smoke mixes, to hold them off.

And, with his visors raised, he could hear something in the sky above. As he looked up, the sky seemed black with the insect-like shapes of Soviet gunships, strafing runs starting across the ground, Rourke accelerating, cutting a wide arc around Natalia and Han, decelerating, braking, skidding the machine to a halt, jumping from it as he put out the stand.

Rourke skidded to his knees beside Natalia and Han Lu Chen, a Scoremaster in each fist. He fired them out through the smoke and clouds of gas toward the advancing Maoist foot soldiers.

"You take Natalia's bike. Get out of here. Head away from here on a tangent to the east. Catch up with the others. I'll be right behind you. I think her weapons systems are exhausted, so just drive like hell."

"I have never—"

"Twist the right hand grip and it's the throttle, work the left side and it's the brakes. Once you catch up, let Maria Leuden drive, you ride behind. Don't let the speedometer get up over sixty and don't try to do anything abruptly. Otherwise, just like riding a horse. Help me with Natalia. Hurry."

Her voice droned on and on in his head, "John—John—"

He was into the saddle, Han balancing Natalia behind him. "Now—Natalia—" He pushed up her visor. "Can you hear me."

Tears streamed from her eyes, the eyes widely dilated, her neck vibrating with her pulse. If she heard him, she didn't know it.

John Rourke had planned ahead, using only half the rope. "Tie her to my shoulders. Hurry!"

Rourke took the rope ends, tied them himself, Han running for Natalia's machine. Rourke pulled down the visor, pushed down hers, strafing runs from above, gunfire from the Chinese troops on the ground. They thought that his attack had been part of the Soviet attack, he realized, gunning the Special.

Han was into the saddle, the Special almost lurching out from beneath him. But Han held on, low over the handlebars, the machine zigzagging maddeningly.

John Rourke spoke into his headset. "Natalia—hold on, darling," and he let the Special out, cutting in behind Han Lu Chen, Han's machine evening out, speeding away, Rourke holding back.

Han was nearly to the edge of the valley, Soviet gunships hovering there, ropes dropping from them, black clad Elite Corps airborne elements rappelling fluidly to the ground.

Han was clear.

Rourke looked back. The only way out lay through the Maoists and Mongols, the way he'd come in.

Rourke checked his fairing mounted guns. Maybe enough ammo. One more package of smoke and gas. The 629, his M-16, the two Detonics Miniguns still loaded.

He whispered to Natalia, so that only she would hear. "And I've always loved you."

She kept crying, moaning his name.

Rourke began to accelerate, working the machineguns in short bursts, the ground around him furrowing under strafing runs from the Soviet gunships above, Maoists and Mongols in front of him and on either side firing handguns and rifles, bullets whining off the fairing, his head reeling, his ears ringing—he realized a bullet had glanced off his helmet. He kept the Special rolling, faster and faster, the digital speedometer at forty now.

A concentration of Mongols closing in behind him on horseback, rifles firing after him. They could hit Natalia. Rourke activated his last smoke and gas package, accelerating now, to sixty, firing his machineguns, firing, firing, the dead falling in waves before him.

A Soviet gunship was directly over him, he realized, machinegun fire on both sides of him, explosions rocking the ground on either side.

He freed his right hand for an instant, drawing the 629, shifting it to his left. He throttled up, the helicopter matching his speed. Rourke rammed the revolver into his belt and braked, the helicopter passing over him, the revolver back in his fist. He stabbed it toward the gunship's underbelly and fired, then again and again, aiming for the rotor now, firing it out, the helicopter veering suddenly to starboard, whether it was hit or not he didn't know.

The revolver into his belt, he gunned the Special ahead, his left hand snatching at one of the mini-guns in the double Alessi rig. A Mongol hurtled himself down from the saddle, Rourke firing into the Mongol's face, the Special bumping up and over the body.

A Maoist officer with an assault rifle, spraying toward them, Rourke's right arm stinging with a grazing hit, the Special wobbling under him. Rourke fired out the little Detonics Combat Master into the officer's chest, then dropped the little pistol into a stowage compartment in the fairing.

The ground was beginning to rise, the rocks ahead. An explosion threw up a shower of dirt and gravel. Rourke accelerated. A Soviet gunship crossed nearly at eye level in front of him and he swerved the Special, accelerated out of the skid, up into the rocks.

Gunfire from the helicopters tore into the rocks around him, the speedometer reading one hundred ten, a straight run ahead now, Rourke accelerating. One hundred twenty. One hundred thirty. One hundred thirty-five.

The ground rippled and furrowed on either side of them, and as he looked up, there were two gunships in pursuit, aerial mines falling, exploding to either side of them, Rourke swerving the machine right and left, recovering just in time to almost lose control again.

One hundred forty.

One forty-five.

The ground was starting to drop off.

His only hope, he had realized since the pursuit had begun moments ago, was to give the gunships nothing to pursue.

He angled the fork left, the ground dropping quickly now, rising steeply ahead. He accelerated, one hundred fifty-two.

The machine, with the added weight of a second rider and the bumpy terrain was almost impossible to control now.

Natalia kept calling his name. "John—"

"I'm here, Natalia," John Rourke whispered.

The ground rose sharply, the terrain slick rock beneath him, high rock walls on either side of him, and suddenly nothing there in front of him.

John Rourke had planned ahead, gunning the last mile per hour of speed out of the Special as it jumped, Rourke's hands leaving the controls, tugging open the knot binding Natalia's body to his, the rushing water of the river fifty feet below, forty, thirty, as he twisted in the saddle, folding Natalia into his arms, then throwing them clear as the machine impacted the turbulent surface, Rourke's body taking the force as the machine broke the water for them, Rourke still holding tight to Natalia as they went under, the water above them exploding under the impacts of machinegun bullets.

CHAPTER THIRTY-FOUR

John Rourke had stripped away her wet clothes, except for her underwear, wrapped her in the disposable insulated blanket he carried in the musette bag. But he could not risk a fire by which to warm her. The radio in his helmet and hers either no longer worked or Annie, Paul and the others were too far out of range to pick up.

His handguns were reloaded, and he would, one at a time, disassemble and clean them, the revolver more challenging in the field like this, but not impossible.

The ammunition he would have to bank on still functioning. But that was the advantage of a knife. It never ran out, and the Crain knife he had wiped down immediately, then left out of the sheath until the sheath began to dry.

He shivered with the cold.

The Special was lost. The sounds of full-scale war still echoed from the Second City miles away, the smoke dense in the distance where the Second City was, Soviet gunships making passes everywhere in the sky above.

They were hidden in a niche of rock, invisible

from the air as best he could discern.

He stripped away his wet clothes and huddled into the blanket with Natalia, her body trembling with cold as he held her to warm her.

They were miles inside hostile territory and, at least here, in the middle of full-scale war, without transportation, without communications, Natalia gravely ill in a state, it appeared, of total mental collapse.

For now, until cover of darkness, there was nothing to do but wait and warm her.

The tears had stopped, but the surrealistically blue eyes only stared vacantly away.

And she kept on repeating his name, her voice hoarse with it now, "John —."